# Nurse's Date with a Billionaire

Pittsburgh

NURSE'S DATE WITH A BILLIONAIRE

ANJ Press, First edition. March 2019.

Copyright © 2019 Amelia Addler.

Written by Amelia Addler.

Cover design by Charmaine Ross at CharmaineRoss.com

*This book is for my mom, who reads everything I've ever written, and my dad, who will definitely hear about this dedication from my mom before he gets to see it with his own eyes.*

*Thank you for showing me what love is.*

# Chapter 1

By her third day working in the ICU, Kali felt prepared for almost anything. She knew where every drug was in the crash cart. She'd memorized the dosages of all the emergency IV drips. In the back of her mind, she kept a history of all of her fellow nurses' lives: their likes and dislikes, the names of their children and pets, and where they liked to go for lunch. But nothing prepared her for the patient in room 13.

He seemed like he'd be an easy patient; he came in after being found down, unconscious, on the street. Despite not waking up once he got to the hospital, there didn't seem to be anything wrong with him. His scans came back negative. No broken bones, no internal bleeding. Blood work stunningly normal. He wasn't even intubated. In truth, he shouldn't have come to the ICU, but they had an open bed and the emergency room doctor insisted. The only thing that was wrong with him was that he wouldn't wake up.

Kali was still vigilant, of course. She'd always been a star nurse, and she didn't want her promotion to the ICU to be any different. And when she left him, just for a moment, to help Ophelia move her patient in room 15, he was completely fine, still totally unconscious, and in no danger whatsoever.

Which is why Kali was surprised and annoyed to hear Betsy calling her after she was away for two minutes. Not wanting to invoke Betsy's wrath, Kali obediently came running out of room 15.

"Yes?"

Betsy crossed her arms. "Kalista, nice of you to come around. Did you not have to keep track of any patients down on the floor?"

She hated when Betsy used her full name. Kali opened her mouth to respond but paused for a moment – this was clearly a sarcastic comment, but she had no idea what prompted it. She also had no idea what prompted someone to unscrew the top of her coffee mug that morning, either, causing half of its contents to spill down her shirt. But such was the way of welcoming her to the unit, it seemed.

"What's going on?" Kali replied, keeping her tone steady and free of snark.

Betsy sighed dramatically and pointed down the hall. Kali followed her finger, catching sight of a hospital gown disappearing behind a corner. She rushed down the hall, muttering an "oh my goodness," under her breath. She watched as the patient, wearing only a hospital gown, approached Dr. Connor and tapped him on the shoulder.

"Pardon me, have you happened to see my trousers?"

Dr. Connor turned to him, a puzzled look on his face. "No sir, I can't say that I have."

"Ah, terrible luck," he said, patting the doctor on the shoulder.

Kali stepped in before he had a chance to say anything else. "Okay now, good to see you up and about, but I need you to go back to your room."

He turned to her, surprised, "Oh hello there! Have you any idea what's happened to my trousers?"

She tried to avoid the glare coming from the nurse's station. "Yes, come with me and I'll explain everything." She placed a hand on his shoulder and tried to guide him back towards his room, but he wiggled away.

"Hang on a minute, I've just – "

"This way, Craig," she said sternly.

"I'm sorry miss, you seem to have the wrong man, I've just popped in for a moment and seem to have gotten turned around."

She stopped, growing increasingly embarrassed that her comatose patient's miraculous recovery led to an immediate escape and an argument in the middle of the ICU. There he stood, barefoot and dangerously close to exposing his backside to everyone, telling her that she *had the wrong man*. She could almost laugh at the absurdity of it, except she knew that Betsy would tell everyone how poorly she handled it and how she *really* didn't belong in the ICU.

He turned to walk away and she took a deep breath. She was not going to be bullied by Betsy. She was a good nurse. And sometimes that meant using her bossy voice.

"You cannot leave the building like that unless you want to freeze to death. Come with me. *Now.*"

He turned to her, his face showing surprise at her change in tone. "No need to get snippy."

She took a firm grip of his shoulder and led him down the hallway.

He continued talking as they walked. "Once we find this Craig fellow, perhaps we can sort out what he did with my trousers."

"Right in here," she said, motioning for him to sit on the bed.

"Oh, no thank you. The blankets are suffocating, to be honest. And the machines in here make quite a racket, I have a terrible headache."

Kali pulled a wheeled computer over. "Do you remember what brought you here?"

He looked around, eyeing the furniture suspiciously. "I can't say that I do."

"Do you know what year it is?"

"Yes of course."

She smiled. "What year is it?"

"2019."

"Good. Do you know what month it is?"

He looked to the window. "February."

"Very good. And your name?"

He opened his mouth, then frowned. "Funny thing, it seems to have slipped my mind."

"Have a seat," she said, "and I'll get the doctor to come over and examine you properly."

"No no, please don't. I don't want them injecting me with something because I can't tell you my name."

She smiled. "Don't worry, he's just going to ask you some questions."

"Really, I'm quite alright, I think I'll be going – "

"Sit!" Kali pointed a finger at him. Frowning, he listened.

She popped her head out into the hallway and waved Ophelia down.

"Hey, can you ask Dr. Connor to come over and tell him that the patient in room 13 woke up?"

"Sure thing!"


Dr. Connor was old school, and Kali knew he'd want to talk to the patient himself. She managed to keep Craig in the room for a few minutes until the doctor arrived.

"Good morning," he said as he came in. "I'm Dr. Connor. I *thought* that was you out in the hall."

"Morning, I'm...Craig."

"Oh! Nice to meet you Craig."

Kali suppressed a smile. Did he really remember his name, or was he just catching on? Dr. Connor spent the next few minutes asking him questions before explaining what was going on more fully.

"Well Craig, if you haven't gathered yet, you had an accident. We're not sure exactly what happened. The paramedics found you down on the sidewalk, your wallet and your shoes were gone, and the only identifying thing you had on you was this."

Dr. Connor handed him a shining money clip.

"Craig's Cash," he read aloud. "Ha! Isn't that clever?"

Kali resisted rolling her eyes. She didn't think it was clever, really, more so pretentious.

"It seems you've suffered some memory loss, and judging from the scrapes and bruises, you've had some head trauma. Nothing serious, but we'll do another scan to make sure there's still no bleeding. No one can be sure how long it will last, but I will say that you otherwise seem remarkably intact. Hopefully it will resolve itself in a few days or weeks."

Craig nodded. "Right. I'm feeling better already. But beg your pardon – where am I, exactly?"

"Madison. Madison, Wisconsin."

"Ah, right," he responded. "That's what I thought."

Dr. Connor smiled. "Any other questions that I can answer?"

"No," Craig said, standing and extending his hand. "You've been *quite* helpful, I hate to be a bother so I will be on my way."

Dr. Connor shook his hand and turned to Kali, lowering his voice. "Let's transfer him out before he tries to walk out of here again."

Kali smiled. "Of course, thank you Dr. Connor." She turned to the computer to finish some documentation.

"Thank you so much for your help, I feel loads better now. I'll just be going – "

"Na-uh," she said, stepping between him and the door. "Have a seat, I'm going to put in for your transfer and then, and only then, will we be able to give you your pants."

"My pants? Ah, alright, trousers. Now Miss...?"

"Kali."

"Miss Kali, it seems I've awoken from my slumber with an accent that suggests this is not home to me."

She nodded. "It does, Craig."

"Do you suppose this is one of those cases where a blow to the head changed my speech? Could I have woken up speaking Vietnamese or fifteenth century Italian?"

"I don't think so, Craig."

"So it is safe to say that I'm very likely English?"

She nodded. "Sounds like it, Craig."

"Right," he said, straightening himself out.

"Let me check with the doctor to see if we can get you some breakfast. Do not let me catch you walking around again."

He smiled cheerily. "Sorry about that!"


Kali left the room but kept a close eye on his door. She got the okay to order breakfast, but since she'd missed the regular ordering time, she called the cafeteria and requested a tray be brought up for him. She put in for his transfer and took a seat at the nurse's station, relieved that she could finally have another sip of coffee.

"No food or drinks in patient care areas," said a stern voice behind her.

She gritted her teeth. "Sorry Betsy, I didn't realize."

"Do you floor nurses regularly eat and drink in front of patients?"

"No," Kali replied evenly, "but we bent the rules a bit because the break room is so far from the nurse's station."

"There's no bending the rules up here. We follow the same rules whether anyone is looking or not."

Kali smiled. "I'll set this away."

Betsy crossed her arms. "And try not to lose your patient again."

"Will do!" Kali replied cheerfully, watching Betsy slowly walk away.

Ophelia popped into the nurses station. "Hey, don't let her get to you."

"She *hates* me."

"She hates everyone," Ophelia replied. "Don't take it personally. How's your guy doing?"

"Seems like he's doing great. He's got a bit of amnesia, though."

"Ah," said Ophelia. "Did the doc think it was drugs? Alcohol?"

"No no," Kali said. "There were no drugs or alcohol in his system. None at all. Dr. Connor said it was probably head trauma."

"Oh! Interesting!"

"Yeah. And get this, he has a full blown British accent."

"No way! Like when people wake up from a coma speaking a different language?"

Kali cocked her head to the side. "That's what he asked. I told him no. I think he's just, you know, British."

"Oh, you're probably right, I guess those are old wive's tales," Ophelia said, laughing.

Kali smiled, still keeping an eye on the door. "I put in for his transfer, so hopefully they can get him to a more suitable floor soon."

"That's good."

"Yeah," Kali said.

"Well I've got to run, but please let me know if you need anything, okay?"

"Thanks Ophelia."

Kali turned back to the computer, trying to focus. She still felt slightly on edge, but tried to calm herself with some facts. Nothing happened to Craig, he was fine. He didn't wander off of the floor or out of the building. Also, it seemed even more likely now that Betsy was the one who loosened the lid on her coffee, likely to teach her a lesson. And third, Craig would soon be transferred out of her unit and out of her life, and she could focus on the next patient who would actually need her help. Hopefully she'd never have to deal with Craig, the great escapist, again.

# Chapter 2

After he was transferred out of the ICU, Craig had to share a room with an elderly man and his nasty cough. He had no interest in catching whatever he had. After one night with him, he made it a point to be ready for the doctor the next morning.

"Good morning Craig, how are you doing today?"

"Hello Dr. Lind! Quite well, thank you. It's all coming back to me pretty rapidly now."

"Is it? That's great news."

"Yeah, I remember it clearly now. Some hooligans confronted me, demanding my wallet. Last thing I remember is a fist coming at me."

"I see. And the headache?"

"Gone. I feel totally fine. And my last name I also remember. It's...Daniel."

"Daniel?"

Oh shoot. Craig realized he'd basically just reversed Daniel Craig's name. He didn't *actually* know what his own last name was – not yet, at least. But he knew who Bond was.

"Daniels," he said hurriedly, stressing the "s" at the end. "I'm staying at a nearby hotel, and I'm sure if I pop in they can help me get a new room key."

"Ah, well that's great news. I'm sure medical records will want to talk to you to correct your chart here...but otherwise, you're good to leave later today."

"Terrific news, thank you so much doctor."

Dr. Lind swiftly exited the room. Craig was surprised how easy it was. How could anyone not tell he was lying? Surely he'd remember who he actually was soon. The sooner the better, obviously, but he didn't need to waste his time being around all of these sick people.

He managed to secure what remained of his clothes. Apparently, his attackers stole not only his wallet, but also his shoes. Must have been nice shoes, he thought ruefully. He needed to secure a new pair before medical records went looking for Craig Daniels – the poor schmuck who would get hit with his hefty bill.

Craig, finally out of his hospital gown, stepped into the hallway to track down his nurse.

"Lisa, do you have a moment?"

She seemed to blush before walking over. "Yes Mr. Smith?"

"Lisa, I'm not sure if you heard, but I just received the excellent news that Dr. Lind said I am good to go. The thing is, my shoes must've been stolen in my attack. Do you have any idea where I might get a loaner pair?"

She beamed. "Yes, of course. We have clothes donated for patients and erm – well, if you could just tell me your size, I can have them send a pair up."

He nodded. He didn't remember his shoe size either. "Right. My size...well, it would be UK sizing. So I'm not sure how to convert it. Perhaps I could make the trip myself and choose a pair?"

"Oh, right, totally forgot!" she giggled.

Craig flashed a smile. He seemed to be having some sort of an effect on her. He couldn't remember if he was good with women – maybe it was his accent?

"It's no trouble," he said. "I'm perfectly capable of walking now. There's nothing wrong with me at all!"

She wagged a finger at him. "I don't think so. Hold on, I'll have someone come up. And you'll need a coat, too?"

"Er – yes, I think so." Right. He was in Wisconsin in the dead of winter for some reason. His assailants stole his coat as well. Craig had the bizarre realization – what if it wasn't a random attack, and he was actually targeted? Had he been committing some sort of crime? Did he *live* a life of crime? Or was he a spy, MI6 agent like Bond? Now wouldn't that be cool.

Truth be told, he had no memory of the attack. He had no memory of what he did for a living or who he was. It was almost amusing – what a fun game it all was.

"Give us some time and we'll get you set up, okay?"

He smiled at her again. "Thanks Lisa."

Craig went back to his room and noticed that his roommate was nowhere to be found. A sound escaped from the restroom, quickly answering the question of what happened to him. Craig frowned in the direction of the door. He decided that a shared room was certainly *not* in his taste. He'd much rather be back in his private, high tech room in the ICU. Even though his nurse there was unimpressed with him.

In fact, she was rather stern. She certainly didn't blush or giggle when he spoke to her; then again, he was still flouncing around in his hospital gown at the time. Perhaps now she'd find him more charming? Eh – probably not. She was stunningly beautiful, so she likely had loads of men wrapped around her finger. One disoriented Brit was not going to charm her.

After about an hour, a volunteer came up to show Craig the various donated articles of men's clothing for him to choose from. He was not pleased with his options. He settled on a pair of slightly worn, but otherwise decent quality leather chukka boots. The coat was more of a problem – every one was a ghastly, poofy parka. Did everyone walk around looking like the abominable snowman in this town? He selected one, noting it appeared to be better suited for skiing, and thanked the volunteer.

Despite feeling a bit bad about it, he decided it'd be best if he scooted out unseen. Hopefully Lisa wouldn't get in too much trouble for not handing him over to the billing people before he left. He was sure that he had money – somewhere, of course. Probably. He could pay after he discovered who he was, but he wasn't going to remember anything while living with a man who was actively coughing out his lung.

Craig kept his head down as he made his way out of the room without being noticed. He walked for a minute until he reached the end of the hall, but wasn't sure where to go from there.

"You look lost, can I help you find where you're going?"

Craig startled, turning to see that the woman sitting behind a desk was addressing him. "Er, yes, thank you. I'm looking for the lift?"

She frowned for a moment, "And where are you trying to go?"

"Just trying to go home," he said, turning towards her so his back faced his old hospital room.

"Oh," she said, letting out a small laugh. "You mean the *elevator*."

"Right, the elevator." How likely was it that he was an international spy if he didn't know what to call the lift in the US? The chance of being a real life Bond was rapidly decreasing.

"Just turn left here, and you'll find the elevator. Take it down to floor two, that's where the lobby is. Don't go down to floor one, that'll take you to the basement."

"Right, thanks again," he said quickly before walking off.

He made it to the lift without incident. He stepped inside, pressed two, and breathed a sigh of relief when the doors closed. He forgot to look around for cameras – surely there weren't cameras everywhere? Perhaps just in the lobby, and it was unlikely anyone noticed he was missing yet.

The doors of the lift opened and he saw his chance to escape – he only had to pass the gift shop and a lightly staffed desk. He stepped into the busy lobby and quickly made his way through, weaving through visitors and employees alike. He got to the door and the glass panes slid open, releasing him into the freezing air.

It was frigid, no doubt about that. He was grateful for his poofy coat now. He then realized that there was a snag in his plan – he didn't know where he was or where he was going quite yet. He considered going back inside to get some information from the person at the front desk, but he decided against it. Surely it would all come back to him now that he was walking around the city again. He headed confidently in the direction that felt best.

After walking for an hour (or more, he had no way to keep track of the time), it seemed like he'd chosen the wrong direction. The buildings thinned out and at times, it was hard to walk alongside the road because the sidewalks disappeared. He saw a group of five people waiting on the sidewalk ahead of him and decided to have a chat with them.

"Excuse me," he said, "can you tell me what you are all waiting for?"

A guy turned to him, slightly puzzled. "We're waiting for the bus."

"Oh! A bus! Lovely. Where does it go?"

"Well," the guy said slowly, clearly suspicious that he was being manipulated in some way, "there's more than one bus."

"Oh, right. Is there one going into town?"

"Downtown?"

"Yes," Craig said, nodding, "downtown."

"Yeah. Should be here soon."

"Ah, lovely." He paused, realizing that he had no money to pay for the bus. "Sorry, one more question – how much is the fare?"

The guy shrugged. "Dunno, I have a bus pass." He took a step away from Craig and put his headphones back into his ears.

Craig stood for a moment. That was going to be a problem. He certainly didn't want to beg for bus fare, but he also didn't want to live the rest of his life at this bus stop.

A bus approached the stop and a few people lined up to get on. It slowed, opening both its front and back doors, and unloaded a handful of people. Craig stood on the sidewalk, lined up with the back door and saw his opportunity – he took a swift step, hopping in and hiding amongst the rest of the standing bus patrons.

The doors closed and the bus lurched forward. There were so many people standing that the bus driver could hardly see what was going on back there. Perfect.

Craig rode along as the landscape changed – more buildings and people out and about. A lot of people got off when they reached Capitol Square, and Craig decided it was as good a time as any to get off of the bus.

It was a very pretty area, and he felt like he'd reached somewhere that might jog his memory. If only someone told him where exactly he was found; he could return there and see if anything looked familiar. Craig felt sure that if he just had a moment to think that he'd remember everything.

His stomach grumbled. It'd been hours since he had breakfast at the hospital, and he walked a good bit. He decided that before he remembered who he was, he needed to find some food.

# Chapter 3

At the end of her shift, Kali swung by the hospital's cafeteria to pick up the unused food. The year prior, she and some of the nurses on her old floor started a program to donate it to a local food bank. They took turns making the deliveries to the food bank, and even though Kali just finished her fourth 12-hour shift of the week, it was her turn and she wasn't going to skip it.

She thought about stopping by her old floor to ask for advice on how to handle Betsy, but apparently there was a recent patient elopement that had everyone in a tizzy. It didn't seem that bad – it sounded as though the patient thought they were okay to leave, so they did, but they didn't get their discharge paperwork or any care coordination. It wasn't as bad as her ICU patient almost escaping. She still got a bad feeling in the pit of her stomach when she thought of it. How could she have let that happen? She so badly wanted to succeed as an ICU nurse, but it felt like everything she did was wrong.

After work, she'd call her mom to unload about the various things that went wrong at work; she'd still worry about them at home, too. No one ever got hurt, but it scared her to even think of how things could go wrong.

It wasn't like Kali was a new nurse; she'd been at it for four years. She got her RN degree when she was 21, then worked as a nurse while attending night school to get her bachelors. Nursing was her life. Other people her age went out and partied; they traveled the world or got married. Kali didn't do any of those things. Her life took a different path.

When she was 19, her high school sweetheart, then fiancé, lost his fight with leukemia. Kali cared for him until his last breath. It forced her to grow up almost overnight, and when he passed away, it felt like her life was over.

She decided not to waste her life, though, and after caring for him, she knew that she needed to become a nurse. She felt a calling from deep in her bones that her purpose was to lessen the suffering of others. Deep down, she knew that she would never love again or get to be married or have kids. But she would be a nurse, and she'd be the best there was.

Except now she wasn't doing so hot. Not wanting to dwell on it, Kali chatted with Marge, the cafeteria manager, and loaded her arms with spare food. It wasn't until after she loaded it into her car and she was halfway to the food bank that Betsy's voice drifted into her head again.

"You act like you've never mixed an IV before," she'd said with a sneer, watching Kali fumble the glass vial of vasopressin.

Kali gritted her teeth remembering it. Of course she'd mixed an IV before. Her hands were tired from doing chest compressions because they were in the middle of a code – a cardiac arrest! Her adrenaline was flowing, it's not like she was incompetent because her hands got a little shaky. The guy lived, though. That was all that really mattered.

She pulled up to the front of the food bank and put on her flash-ers; it never took long for her to run the food inside. Kali ran back into the kitchen; everyone knew her there, and she yelled a hello before dropping the food off and rushing back to the front doors.

There were a lot of people milling about the food bank that evening. The staff prepared some hot meals for people as well, which always made it a popular spot when the weather got so cold. Kali smiled at everyone as she walked through, feeling guilty that she didn't volunteer more often to actually serve food.

She was almost at the front door when she saw a familiar face. She stopped, trying to think where she knew him from.

He saw her looking at him and said, "Fancy seeing you here! I thought they'd pay you nurses a bit more fairly so you could afford a meal, heaven knows you deserve it."

She couldn't help but crack a smile. It was her British escapee patient. "Hi Craig, it's nice to see you. I was just dropping off some food from the hospital."

"These poor people," he said, lowering his voice, "aren't even *in* hospital and you're going to inflict that food on them anyway?"

In hospital. Was that how British people said "in the hospital?" Or did he actually have a head injury? "Oh come on, the food isn't that bad."

He laughed. "No, I just had the stew and it was quite agreeable."

"Oh, that's good. Is your memory almost back to normal?"

He frowned. "Do you know – it isn't really. Still figuring out exactly what happened that night."

"Oh," she replied.

"And what my last name is," he added with a laugh.

Oh shoot. Here Kali assumed he was back to his normal life – that maybe he fell on hard times and was living in the shelters. He certainly didn't *look* like someone on hard times. True, he had on a ridiculous jacket, but the color made his blue eyes pop. Plus, he was an extremely handsome man, all sharp jawed and rugged with just a bit of stubble. With his tall and muscular build, he certainly didn't fit the profile of someone scraping by on the streets.

"So you...don't know where home is, still?" she asked carefully.

He shook his head, rubbing a hand on his chin. "Not yet. I'm hoping it'll come back to me soon enough."

"Oh," she said again. "Well...did one of the social workers set you up with a place to stay?"

"They can do that?" he sounded surprised.

"I think so – maybe? Or they may have gotten you into the men's shelter?"

"Ah, yes, the men's shelter," he said, leaning back. "They're ah – out of beds at the moment. Terrible luck."

"That's awful!" she said without thinking. It was awful, though. Where was he supposed to go? The man had no memory, no money and no options. How could the hospital have just sent him out like that? It was so out of character for one of their social workers to drop the ball like that.

"It's alright," he said quickly, almost as though he knew what she was thinking. "No one is at fault. It seemed like I got there just when they ran out of space. You know, bad weather and all."

"Sure," she said.

She didn't have time to have a long conversation. Her car was parked in an unloading only zone, plus she was exhausted from her shift and needed to get home. Also, it wasn't her job to figure out where this guy could go stay. But...

Maybe she wasn't thinking clearly because she was so tired, but this guy was going to *freeze to death* if he had nowhere to go. How could she let that happen?

She bit her lip, thinking about how she'd only recently finished the basement of her small townhouse and turned it into a simple, but useful, studio apartment. Her plan was to put it up on Airbnb to rent for some extra money. The only thing she hadn't gotten around to yet was getting a lock on her side of the basement door to keep visitors out of her living space.

Logically, it seemed it would be reasonable for him to stay there so he didn't freeze to death. Yet her anxiety chimed in and reminded her that not having a lock on the door made it dangerous, especially if he was actually a lying psychopath who decided to come up and murder her.

"If you know any other places, I'm all ears," he said.

"Hold on a second," she said, unable to work through the very bad idea that was forming in her head. She struggled between anxious thoughts of him freezing to death and her car currently being towed.

Kali stepped past him and went out to her car. She was happy to see that it was still sitting there, un-towed, and she took a deep breath to clear her head.

This was a bad idea. She knew it was a bad idea. First of all, she didn't know this guy. She lived alone. If he attacked her, she would end up on the local news as the woman who stupidly picked up a strange man at the food bank and suffered the obvious consequences. Then again, she kind of *did* know him. Just a few days ago, he was in a coma. He had no memory of his life – so Kali was one of the only people who knew anything about him.

Second, if the hospital found out that she allowed a patient to stay in her apartment, even as a renter, she would  be fired immediately. They frowned on anyone forming inappropriate relationships with prior patients or their families; becoming a landlord to a former patient would *definitely* be inappropriate.

But he had nowhere to go. It was going to snow again tonight and the temperature would stay well below zero. He had no plan, and if he wandered out into the night, they'd find him the next morning frozen solid like a popsicle. And she would have his life on her hands, because she could've prevented his death, but instead she did nothing.

Kali closed her eyes and tried to think. She needed to push away her anxiety about the situation and do the right thing. All she needed to do was employ her most stern nurse voice and let him know that she wasn't messing around. She'd developed the voice after years of working as a nurse – it was almost funny to her, because before that, she was the most shy and meek person on earth. She still had trouble being assertive outside of work sometimes. But not when she was in nurse mode.

She walked back into the food bank. "Alright, listen Craig."

He turned to her, a surprised look on his face. "Yes?"

"I have somewhere you can stay, just until you regain your memory."

"Oh, that's great!"

She lowered her voice. "I have an apartment that I was going to rent out, but I'll make an exception on the rent for you."

He started speaking again but she cut him off. "*However,* if you are destructive, aggressive, or uncooperative to any degree, you are out. If you so much as sneeze in a way that makes me uncomfortable, you are out. Are we clear?"

He nodded. "Yes, got it. Creepy behavior is punishable by death."

She frowned. "I'm not joking, Craig."

"Of course not! I understand and you have my promise that I'll behave in a most gentlemanly manner."

Kali decided to leave it there. "Alright, let's go."

He followed her outside and she unlocked her car's doors. He motioned to open the passenger's door in the front and she hesitated for a moment. Should she make him sit in the back like she was running a cab service? Or would that be weird?

It was too late, he already got in. She sighed and walked over to the driver's side.

"I'd offer to drive," he said, "but I'm not sure that I know how."

"That's fine," she answered before turning on the car and pulling away from the curb.

He kept talking. "So, what brings you to Madison? Did you grow up here?"

"No. I grew up about a half hour north of here."

"Ah. Well, let me tell you what brought *me* to Madison."

She kept her eyes on the road. "Yeah?"

He was silent for a few moments. "Oh, didn't work. I hoped that would force me to remember something."

She ignored him. Was he trying to crack jokes to lower her guard? It wasn't going to work.

Out of the corner of her eye, she saw his hand extend towards her, causing her to flinch.

"Sorry!" he said, snapping his hand back. "Just wanted to turn up the radio."

"Oh, go ahead." Relax, Kali. He's not going to kill you while you're driving him around. He'll at least wait until you stop the car.

He continued chatting for the rest of the fifteen minute drive and Kali kept her answers short. She needed him to know that she was serious about him not breaking any rules. She'd have no choice but to kick him out if he did something weird.

They arrived at her apartment and she parked on the street.

"Oh, this looks nice," he remarked.

She ignored him and led him to the side door that worked as a private entrance for the basement apartment.

"This way," she said.

"Oh dear," he said, following behind her, "this isn't one of those Sweeney Todd type basements, is it? Am I on my way to becoming one of those vagrants you see on the news?"

Kali almost cracked a smile but managed to stop it. "I hate to break it to you, Craig, but you're already kind of off the grid. No one knows that you're here."

"You're right," he said with a fake gasp. "A perfect victim, really."

She looked at him, holding a key in the door. "Do you prefer to sleep outside, then?"

He answered immediately. "You know, I like you. I think I'm going to go with my gut on this one and put my life in your hands."

"Again, you mean?" she replied.

"Well I didn't have much of a choice the first time, did I?"

Kali turned away from him and opened the door, rolling her eyes where he couldn't see. She flicked on the light.

"It's not much, but it's cozy."

"It's brilliant!" he said, striding in behind her. "I feel like I just walked into a little cabin in the woods."

"Yeah, thanks," Kali said, a bit gruffly. In truth, she was quite pleased with how the basement apartment turned out. She spent a lot of time figuring out how to remodel the small space to make it passable as a studio. Her dad and brother helped with a lot of the manual labor, and she spent countless days popping in and out of thrift stores to find just the right decorations to give it a cozy feel. Craig didn't need to know all of that, though. He needed to know he couldn't flatter his way out of behaving responsibly.

Craig took off his coat and set it on a nearby chair before walking around slowly to look more closely at a painting on the wall. Kali caught herself looking at him for a moment too long – she'd only ever seen him in the poofy coat or in a hospital gown. He was wearing a black t-shirt now, though, and he was wearing it well. She realized she was staring at his broad shoulders and brawny arms. Clearly he wasn't a vagrant – no one maintains muscles like *that* while underfed.

No, whoever he was in his real life, Craig clearly worked out and took care of himself. It also meant that he could easily overpower her. She reminded herself of this and cleared her throat.

"I'll run upstairs and bring down some food for you, in case you're hungry. I'm not sure what I have, but…"

"Oh no, I'm alright. Thank you for the offer, though. Is your husband…?"

"No," she said a little too quickly. Shoot, he didn't need to know that she lived alone. As much as he joked about *her* being a threat to *him*, he was clearly the more threatening one with his crazy gym muscles.

"My – roommate won't mind," she added. She didn't have a roommate, but he didn't need to know that. "It's my townhouse. We share a wall with the owners of the townhouse next door, though. So be sure to keep it quiet."

"You got it, boss. Forgive me, but is this a painting of the Eiffel tower?"

"Yes, you recognize it? Have you ever been?"

He stared at it for a moment. "I feel that I have, but I can't be sure. Have you?"

"No. Not yet. Someday, though."

He smiled. "Ah, Paris est une belle ville!"

"You speak French?"

He made a face as though he was impressed with himself. "Apparently, I do."

She looked around for a moment. "Alright, well, towels are in the bathroom. You can help yourself to the tea or whatever is in the kitchen. The TV should work, too. And, uh, have a good night."

"Thank you Kali. You too."

It wasn't exactly how she dreamed her first rental of the studio would go, but oh well. Kali went up the stairs, closing the door behind her and making a big show of locking the door that separated the basement staircase from her kitchen. The lock was broken, but he didn't need to know that. She shoved a door stop under the door so it wouldn't open easily. Just in case.

As much as she thought it'd be impossible to sleep with a stranger downstairs, Kali was too exhausted to even think about it. Her first week in the ICU wiped her out. She laid down in her bed and within a minute, dozed into a heavy sleep.

# Chapter 4

Craig listened as Kali walked up the stairs and locked the door behind her. He thought joking about Sweeney Todd would make her feel more comfortable – to sort of point out that he knew it was odd for her to take a strange man into her home. But after he said it, he realized that it might've made her feel worse.

He rubbed his forehead. Hopefully he wouldn't need to inconvenience her too long. He was more than grateful that she offered him a place to stay. This place was *loads* better than the men's shelter. He made a tiny, little white lie that the shelter was full. They never *said* they were full. But Craig took one look at the place and turned around. It looked pretty full anyway. He decided he'd rather freeze to death than spend a night there. Somehow it was even worse than his hospital room with the dying man.

After inspecting the space, he decided to take a shower. He stared at himself in the mirror for a few minutes before getting undressed. It was like looking at a stranger. His face looked vaguely familiar, like someone he knew long ago, but he couldn't have picked himself out of a lineup if he needed to. It was too uncanny to stare at his reflection; he turned on the shower and stepped into the hot water. Kali left some rather sweet smelling shampoo and soaps that made the experience thoroughly enjoyable.

After toweling off, he settled into bed. It, too, was luxurious in it's own way, the blankets with just enough weight to make him feel wrapped up without feeling overheated. Despite wanting to stay up to try to remember something about who he was, he quickly slipped into a dreamless sleep.

The next morning he awoke naturally; there wasn't much sunlight coming into the basement. He could hear a lot of activity above him – Kali was walking around, the floor creaking beneath her, and he could somewhat make out her voice talking in a high pitch. She seemed to be talking to an animal or a small child. He smiled to himself – even beautiful, stern Kali let her guard down sometimes.

He got dressed, feeling a bit annoyed that he didn't have another set of clothes. The homeless shelter gave him a small bag with basics the night before – socks, underwear, and little packs of tuna and granola bars. At least he had some fresh undergarments, but getting anything new would be difficult without money.

He knew he had money – somewhere, he must have a bank account. It might just be a few days until he could access it. Not knowing his own name was a bit of a hurdle.

He made his way up the stairs and knocked quietly on the door. He heard Kali stop moving.

"Yes?" she called out.

"Morning," he responded. "I was wondering if I could have a word with you."

He heard her walk towards the door before opening it a crack. "Okay?"

He cleared his throat. "I promise I don't bite."

She sighed, apparently weighing the risk of letting him inside versus having to ignore him all day. She opened the door.

He smiled and took a step into the kitchen. She closed the door behind him.

"I heard you speaking to someone up here? Was it your...room-mate?"

"No, I was feeding the cats."

"You have cats?"

Kali nodded, stooping down to pick up two small bowls from the ground.

"You have two cats?"

"No," she said, rinsing the bowls in the sink. "They're not mine, they're foster cats. They're just staying with me until they're adopted."

Craig leaned to peer into the next room, spying a large rectangular cage on the ground and a tall bird cage, fluttering with activity, above it.

"And those?"

"Oh. Foster ferrets. And budgies. I take any overflow animals from the shelter. They don't have enough room to keep them all the time, especially in the winter."

"I see. So along with homeless people, you host homeless animals as well."

"That's right," she said dryly.

"I thought I dreamed up the menagerie up here, I had no idea that you were running such an operation."

She leaned against the counter and crossed her arms. "What did you want to talk to me about?"

"Ah, right, well – "

"Did you come up here for breakfast?"

"No, actually, the shelter provided me with some courtesy tuna. I'm happy to share it with you, in fact, I find room temperature tuna to give a great start to the day."

"Ugh, gross," she said, cracking a smile. He liked those rare smiles.

"Your loss. No, I have a proposition for you."

She raised an eyebrow. "Oh really?"

"Yes. You might've noticed that I'm having trouble recovering my memories."

She nodded.

"I really thought that they'd be back by now," he continued, "but they just aren't. So I find myself in this grand predicament where I don't have an identity, or any means to discover it."

"Right," she said slowly.

"And the thing is, I must have a past. I'm sure I have a life some-where, but until I can find it, I'm sort of out of luck."

She stared at him. "Clearly."

He smiled. "See, I can tell you're really not buying into this, so I think I can safely say that I'm not a salesman in my real life."

A half smile formed on Kali's lips, but she said nothing.

"Hear me out. I'd like to arrange to take a small loan from you, just enough to buy another set of clothes, perhaps, and to arrange transportation on the bus. We can put it in writing, and once my memories return, I'll return the money with whatever interest rate you choose."

"Sounds like you might've been a banker in your past life," she replied.

"Hm." He paused. "No, that doesn't sound right. But I like the idea, keep them coming!"

She rubbed her forehead. "How much money are you talking?"

"Literally as close to nothing as possible. Perhaps a month bus pass, a few more shirts and the like. And of course, I can reimburse you for any petrol that we use in acquiring these things."

"Petrol..." she repeated. "Right. And an interest rate that I set? Two hundred percent?"

"Sure. I assure you that I plan to inconvenience you as little as possible. I'd like to walk the area where I was found, to see if it triggers any memories. Hopefully that'll do the trick."

"Do you know where you were found?"

"Ah, I will also be needing your expertise for this. I'm not sure how I was even brought to the hospital."

Kali frowned. "I see."

She wasn't agreeing to anything, but at least she was listening. He took it as a good sign. "Also, I'll be glad to repay you the full cost of renting the room."

"And if you never regain your memory?"

Craig paused. The thought hadn't even crossed his mind. Surely that couldn't be possible? Surely someone was looking for him?

"I'm sorry, that was mean," Kali said, softening her tone.

"No, you're right," he said. "I just...hadn't considered it."

"Oh," she said.

"I'd like to think of myself as a positive person," he said with a wink. "It's easy to do when I don't know who I am."

"Good point." She laughed. "So, you want to go to the thrift store and get some cheap clothes? And then find out where the ambulance picked you up?"

"Yes," he replied. "And I'd like to return there. I think it'd help."

Kali stood for a moment, studying him. "Well – I'm off for the next two days. From work. I guess I can help you poke around a bit."

"Really? That's brilliant!"

"I need some coffee first, though," she said, pouring herself a cup. "Would you like some?"

"Sure."

"Milk and sugar?"

He crossed his arms. "I don't know."

"Oh, right," she said. "Well, try this and tell me if it tastes good to you."

He took a sip of the coffee and made a face. "That's...not good at all."

She laughed, pulling open the fridge door to grab milk. "Try it with this."

He poured in some milk and took another taste. "Oh, much better."

"Good," she said, busying herself with cleaning up the kitchen.

"Can I help with that?"

"Uh, no, that's fine. I need to get ready so just, uh, stay here. I'll be back in a minute."

He obediently didn't move from his seat, swiveling only to get a better look at one of the cats who emerged from hiding to give him a dirty look.

After a few minutes, Kali reemerged with a laptop. She also changed out of her hooded sweatshirt and into a t-shirt. Craig couldn't help but look at her. Before this, he'd only seen her dressed in bulky scrubs, and she was gorgeous even then. Now he had to force himself not to stare at her. Though he obviously couldn't remember all of the women he'd seen in his life, he was sure that she was one of the most beautiful women he'd ever seen with his own eyes.

He cleared his throat and motioned to the laptop. "What's this for?"

"For you. I'm going to find the phone numbers for some of the local ambulance companies and see who brought you in."

"Oh, brilliant."

They spent the next half hour making calls until they got their answer: Craig was found down at the edge of James Madison park, on the corner of North Butler and East Gotham streets.

"That sounds ominous," Craig said. "Is that Gotham like, Batman's Gotham? Did Batman attack me?"

She stared at him, a blank look on her face. "I think you may be onto something."

Craig nodded. "I knew it. Shall we head out and find him then?"

Kali sighed. "Alright, sure."

He considered opening the front door for her, but thought it might be overkill. People didn't do things like that nowadays, did they? She'd probably think that he was gunning to steal her car. He settled for taking the front seat and not making any sudden movements towards the radio.

It only took a few minutes to get into town, and Kali was excited to find a parking spot on a street a block away from the park. Craig was impressed by how smoothly she parallel parked, but decided to keep it to himself. No need to be a brown noser; he looked out the window to see if anything jogged his memory.

As soon as Kali stepped out of the car, a truck pulled wildly in front of her. Engine still running, a large, red-faced man charged towards her. Craig only realized what was going on when he heard the man yelling.

"You stole that spot out from under me!" screamed the man. "And you hit my truck doing it!"

He gesticulated to a large indentation on the side of the truck bed. Craig hurriedly undid his seatbelt and got out of the car.

Kali took a step back. "I don't think my car is even tall enough to, uh – "

The man poked Kali hard, forcing her to fall backwards.

Craig felt a flash of rage burn through his chest. He'd had enough of this fellow.

# Chapter 5

Kali fell into the side of her car. She couldn't believe that a single poke could dislodge her like that – looking down, she realized she'd slipped on some ice. She coughed, trying to recover after the air was knocked out of her lungs.

That never happened to her before – not in real life anyway, except one time in high school gym class when a game of flag football got out of hand and she landed flat on her back. Even with her most violently delirious patients, she'd always managed to get by without too much damage.

A second later, she saw the blur of Craig's jacket rushing towards her attacker. Though the man was fairly large, Craig was taller and clearly faster, and in a moment had him by the scruff of his jacket.

"That's quite enough," Craig said firmly, holding the man immobilized against his own truck.

"Get off me!" he yelled, struggling to free his hands. One arm broke free and a flailing elbow landed square on Craig's eye.

Craig calmly grabbed the man's arm and pinned it back to his side. "Not so easy with someone your own size, is it?"

Kali came to her senses and straightened up. "Craig – let him go!"

He peered back over his shoulder at her. "Are you sure? I can hold him here 'til the police arrive."

"Are you kidding me?" the guy called out, squirming angrily in Craig's firm grip. "You're gonna call the police over this? I'll sue you!"

Craig turned back to him. "*You're* going to sue *me*? After coming at us, ranting and raving, then assaulting a lady? Luckily our dash camera caught your whole saga on video. Bravo, it'll be an award winner."

The man stopped struggling and his tone quickly changed. "Please, let me go, this is all a big misunderstanding."

Craig loosened his grip, patting the man playfully on the shoulder. "Is it? That's funny, because I also heard you accuse us of hitting your truck in a spot that we couldn't possibly have reached with our little car."

"You're right," he stammered, rubbing his neck with one hand. "My mistake."

"Can I see your phone?" asked Craig gently, turning to Kali.

She nodded, still a bit in shock, and pulled her phone out of her back pocket. She watched as Craig took a picture of the man and his license plate.

"Good. Now if we return to our car and anything is amiss, I'll know who to contact," he said lightly, as though he were making plans for dinner.

"Yeah yeah," the guy said, walking back to his car. "Crazy Irishman," he muttered.

Craig turned to Kali in surprise. "Did he just call me an Irishman? He'll clearly have a hard time identifying me in court. Then again, maybe *someone* can identify me in court, it'd be quite the help really."

Kali watched as the man got back into his truck and drove off.

"Are you alright?" Craig said, taking a step towards her.

She cleared her throat. "Yes...yes, I'm fine."

"Are you *really* alright? Let me get you a coffee. Or a hot cocoa. You can put it on my tab."

She let out a small laugh. "No, it's alright. I'm okay. I guess I just – I was stunned. I didn't know how to react. I'm not usually...easily surprised."

It was true. She'd dealt with so much craziness at work that she almost expected it. One lumbering idiot in a truck, though, and she reverted back to being a quiet and meek girl. Kali felt disgusted with herself. How could she have let that man literally push her around?

"Hey, it's okay. You weren't expecting to be assaulted just then. Happens to the best of us."

She nodded quickly. "It looked like he got you pretty good, let me see your face."

Craig leaned down and Kali removed her glove, gently touching the skin around his eye. He flinched.

"Sorry," she said.

"Oh, that's nothing. I used to get punched all the time in my old life."

"Really?"

"I have no idea," he said, stooping to pick up some snow to press to his face. "But it sounded like it fit, didn't it?"

Kali laughed a little too hard. She felt the tension of the situation easing up. "It did."

"You don't happen to have a dash camera, do you?"

Kali shook her head. "No. But that was some quick thinking. It really made him change his tune."

"Yes, it really did." He threw the snow back on the ground. "Not entirely sure where I came up with that. Well then, would you like to just go back home and have a rest?"

"No, I'm okay. Really. Let's walk around and see what you remember."

"Are you sure you're not hurt?"

"I'm tougher than I look," Kali replied, dusting the snow off of the back of her coat.

"Alright, if you insist."

They walked to the corner of the park where the ambulance found Craig.

"Anything look familiar?" Kali asked.

He frowned. "Sadly, no. Not yet. I wonder what I was doing down here, wandering around the park at night."

"That's the question of the week," Kali replied.

They walked through the park, Craig admiring the view of the lake and asking if the two lakes ever flooded the area. It seemed oddly insightful and Kali wondered if he were an engineer or something. She didn't mention anything to him, though. She didn't want him to feel smug about being insightful. He was already annoying her with his potential made up identities.

"First I thought I was MI6," he said as they strolled down Gotham.

"Like James Bond?"

"Yeah. But then I didn't know what you people call a lift, so it seemed unlikely that I was an international spy."

She nodded. "Definitely."

"Then I got a bit worried I led some sort of life of crime, but that doesn't make sense because I don't think my assailants would've let me live if I were a criminal, and they were criminals too."

"Right."

"Now I'm leaning towards something a bit more heroic, like a firefighter or a window cleaner."

Kali sputtered out a laugh. "How is a window cleaner heroic?"

"Dunno, I saw some blokes yesterday scaling the side of a building to clean some windows. It was freezing and they rode up in this tin can looking thing. Seemed pretty brave to me."

Kali caught him shooting her a look, clearly trying to see if he could get her to laugh. She walked ahead of him, shaking her head. It was harder and harder to take him seriously, and after he saved her, she felt a bit indebted to him, which she found annoying. She didn't like owing anyone anything. He was still a stranger. A stranger that she shouldn't allow to live in her house for a number of reasons, not the least of which that he was a former patient and she was breaking about a hundred rules. She kept her responses short so he didn't get any ideas that they were friends.

After an hour of walking around, Kali stopped to suggest that they take a break. Craig didn't respond – he was standing frozen in front of a diner.

"Are you...hungry?" she asked.

He shook his head, pointing at the sign. "Maggie's Diner!"

Kali looked at the sign, then back at him. "Okay?"

"Maggie's Diner! I took a picture of this place!"

"Oh really? You remember that?"

"Yeah! I remember doing it! I was excited, I wanted to show it to someone."

"Who?"

He paused. "I'm not sure."

"Oh." Her voice fell. "Well, I guess that's a start."

He stood for a moment, staring at the sign. "Maybe someone I knew liked the diner."

"Or their name is Maggie," Kali suggested. Like his sister, or mother. Or wife.

"Can we pop inside, just to see if anyone remembers me?"

"Sure," she said.

They walked into the diner and stood by the "Please Wait To Be Seated" sign. After a minute, a rosy cheeked girl came over.

"Just two?" she said.

"Er – no, actually," said Craig. "I'm actually in a bit of a predicament where I'm suffering from a bit of amnesia. I recognized this restaurant and was wondering if, on an off chance, anyone here knows me?"

The girl blushed a deep red. "Well I'm sure I've never seen you before, but let me check!"

"Thank you," Craig said, smiling at her.

Kali's eyes darted between the girl and Craig. She was clearly fawning over him. Maybe Craig used his good looks to manipulate women. Kali straightened and zipped her jacket all the way up. He wasn't going to manipulate her.

"Are you cold?" he asked, noticing her hand still holding the zipper, which was now up to her chin.

"No, why?"

"No reason," he said, looking away.

After a moment, the girl came back, somewhat recovered from her blush, but her skin was still splotchy with redness. "I'm sorry, sir, but no one here thinks they've seen you before. Maybe check back this weekend? We'll have our weekend crew here."

He smiled graciously. "Oh, right. Thanks for your help."

"You're welcome! Come back soon!"

He nodded and turned to leave. Kali followed him, and once they were out on the sidewalk she spoke again.

"Sorry Craig."

"It's alright," he said, voice low. "I suppose it was silly to think that walking around town would lead to me remembering everything at once."

Kali bit her lip. He was clearly sad. Understandably, of course, but she struggled with how to respond. If he were still her patient in the hospital, she'd offer support and encouragement. She might even hold his hand or put an arm around him.

But not now. She had to be the stern landlady. She didn't want to be suckered by him if he was some great con artist.

"How about," she said slowly, "we give your brain a rest and get you some new clothes? Then I can make us something for lunch. Your basement apartment doesn't have an oven, if you didn't notice."

"Oh," he said lightly, "I don't think I did. I was so focused on that tuna this morning."

She smiled. "Alright then, let's go."

They headed back towards the car, Kali feeling a bit anxious about what they might find. She couldn't help but say something.

"What if the truck guy came back and smashed all of the windows?"

"Then we'll sweep up all of the glass and kindly return it to his truck," Craig said. "We can break one of his windows if needed."

Kali narrowed her eyes at him. "Maybe you did lead a life of crime."

He laughed. "Don't think so. That doesn't appeal to me one bit."

"Unlike window washing?"

"Right," he said.

They arrived at the car and found it in one piece. Kali breathed a sigh of relief as she climbed into the driver's seat. It took about fifteen minutes to get to the shopping plaza that had the thrift store. Craig eyed it from outside.

"Doesn't look like much, does it?"

"I'm keeping your tab low. Let's go."

He sighed. "Alright."

Craig proved to be a poor shopper. He lost interest in clothing easily and continuously wandered over to the aisles with games, house supplies and toys.

"What is this?" he asked, delighted, standing over a child's play kitchen.

"It's a play set," Kali told him patiently.

"It's a *tiny* kitchen! Look at this little pan! And this miniature oven!"

She shook her head. "Did you want to get another pair of pants, or do you want to just live in that one pair for the rest of your life?"

Craig shook his head wistfully. "What a terrific little shop. Alright, my apologies, I'll return to the trousers."

Eventually, Kali managed to corral him into buying a week's worth of clothing, plus some gloves and a hat, since he didn't get any of that when given his coat.

Craig stopped to examine some coats, debating the merits of the one he currently had. "While it *is* horrendous, it's acceptably warm

AMELIA ADDLER

and functional. Plus, I don't want to run up my tab any more than I need to at this point."

Kali shrugged. "Alright."

They checked out, the total coming to $23. Craig insisted on keeping the receipt so he could keep track of what he owed her. "And," he said, "we should keep a running log as well. How much is it to rent the cottage?"

She laughed. The cottage. It was just a basement with some twinkle lights hung up. "Ah – I don't know yet. Let me think about it."

"Very good," he replied.

They walked back to the car, and Kali was glad to see that his mood recovered. Well, mostly glad. He was back to his chatty self, trying his best to get a laugh out of her. She kept her eyes on the road as she drove, but when he did a full reenactment of the truck guy's whining, she did crack a smile.

42

# Chapter 6

They arrived back at Kali's townhouse and Kali offered to let him use the washer and dryer to wash all of his new clothes. Craig stood in front of the machines for five minutes, unable to figure out which one was the washer. He poked the dials, but nothing happened.

"Kali," he called out, "I hate to trouble you while you're cooking, but which of these do I use first?"

Kali appeared with a furrowed brow. "You knew how to use my phone to take a picture but you can't remember how to use a washing machine?"

"I guess not."

She pointed to the one on the left. "This is the washer." She threw his pile of clothes in.

"Ah, right. Of course," he said, nodding solemnly.

"You turn this dial here...okay now the water is coming in. And here is the detergent."

"Right," he said, accepting the bottle. "And...where does this go?"

She looked at him for a moment to see if he was joking. He wasn't. "Just dump it in there. With the clothes."

"Yes yes, it's all coming back to me now."


It wasn't. Craig didn't know how much detergent to add, so he just tilted the bottle, counted to five, then stopped pouring.

"Do I need to close this lid?" he called out.

"Yes!" Kali yelled back.

That seemed to make sense. He closed the washer and placed the detergent bottle on top before making his way back to the kitchen. On his way, he took a detour into the small family room, where the TV, couch, and caged animals were.

The walls were scattered with pictures big and small. Craig paused to look at them and wonder who the smiling faces were.

"Is this your mum and dad here?"

Kali strained her neck to see what he was looking at. "Yep."

"And this is you, isn't it?" He pointed to a picture with four beaming children.

"Yeah."

"A brother and two sisters?"

"Yep," she replied.

"I wonder if I have any siblings," Craig said, staring at the picture intently. They all looked vaguely alike. Kali was the oldest – though he could've guessed that with the way she carried herself. The youngest two girls appeared to be twins.

He moved onto the other pictures and found one of Kali, maybe 18 or so, with a young man. He didn't look like a relative. His hair was sandy blonde, a stark contrast to Kali's dark chestnut color. His face was attractive, for sure, but shared no features with the four siblings in the other picture.

Craig stole a glance at Kali darting around the kitchen. Who was this guy? There didn't seem to be any more recent pictures of him. It seemed odd, but Craig felt like it was inappropriate to ask for some reason.

"Are you sure I can't help with something?" he said, returning to the kitchen.

"I'm sure, can't have you burning the house down."

"Hey," he said, "I know which of these appliances is the oven. It's that one." He pointed at the fridge.

She rolled her eyes.

He smiled broadly. "What, nothing? I thought that was pretty good."

"You can set the table," she said.

"Fantastic!" He felt eager to busy himself and after opening all of the cupboards, he found the plates. "Are we having soup? Salad?"

"I have chicken soup if you like," Kali replied, "and yes to the salad."

Craig located some cloth napkins in a drawer next to the utensils. He folded the napkins and placed them on the plates, then placed bowls on top. He put the salad and dinner forks to the left of the setting, then the knife to the right. He took the smaller plates and set them in the upper left with butter knives overtop. He carefully adjusted everything to make sure it was even.

He didn't notice that Kali stood behind him, staring.

"I hope this is alright. I need to find your glasses..."

"Where did you learn to do that?" she said, setting down a large bowl of salad.

"Do what?"

"Set a table like a waiter in a...I don't even know where. Some fancy restaurant."

He looked at the table and shrugged. "How else would you set a table?"

She looked at him for a moment. "Right," she said, mimicking his accent.

He thought it was a poor imitation, but he let it slide.

Craig looked back at the table. Had he set it correctly? He didn't even think about where everything went. Maybe his memory was coming back in pieces. Pieces centered around household chores (excluding washing clothes) and dingy looking diners.

They sat down, and Craig was thoroughly impressed with the meal that Kali threw together so effortlessly. "This looks simply wonderful," he said.

She passed him the plate of chicken. "It's just chicken soup. And some chicken cutlets. Notice the heavy rotation of chicken in this meal."

"The chef is so humble, too," he replied, smiling.

"It's easy to impress a man whose only memories of food are from the hospital, and a can of tuna from a homeless shelter."

He raised two fingers. "Two cans of tuna."

"Two cans? For breakfast? You're going to get mercury poisoning!"

He frowned. "You're right, I should have demanded that you make me some of these chicken cutlets instead."

"Ha ha."

He stole a glance at her. She was kind of smiling. "Do you often cook for others? Is your roommate going to join us?"

"Oh – uh, no she's busy."

He nodded. He hadn't seen much of this mysterious roommate yet, but Kali clearly didn't want him prying into her personal life. He'd already taken over her basement and her washing machine, he knew it was best not to push his luck.

Kali's phone rang. She leapt up to grab it so quickly that she startled Craig.

"Sorry, it's work," she said.

"Please, don't mind me," he said, nodding towards the phone.

Kali looked at the phone and frowned. "Hi Betsy. What's up?"

Craig stole a glance at her. Her brow was furrowed – already worried about whatever this was.

"Yes, I'm having a nice day off."

A pause. Kali rubbed her forehead.

"Uh, sorry Betsy," she said slowly, "I don't think I can do that many overnights on such short notice."

Craig looked at her again. She continued to listen for a few moments before saying goodbye.

After making her way back to the table, she went to set her phone down, but then gasped.

"What's the matter?" Craig asked, staring at her intently.

"My coworker...or someone...must've seen us out today. Look." She handed him the phone. It was a picture of them walking around downtown together, clear as day.

"Would you look at that, we've been papped. Bit of a weird hobby for your colleague."

Kali groaned. "She's using it to make me cover a bunch of overnight shifts. I can't *believe* this!"

"What, you're not allowed to walk around with men unsupervised or something?"

Kali shook her head. "Not when they're my former patient. It's considered...immoral, in a way."

Craig cocked his head to the side. "Why? We haven't done anything improper."

"That's not the point!" Kali tossed the phone on the table and went into the living room.

"Hold on," Craig said, rising from his chair to follow her. "What if I had a job? And I rented the room from you? That would make it all above board."

"How are you going to get a job?"

"I have my ways," he said, raising an eyebrow.

"Life of crime again?"

Craig crossed his arms. "No, I'm serious."

She sighed. "I don't know if it would matter, honestly. I'm probably breaking a bunch of ethics rules anyway."

"How is that possible? You saved me from freezing to death. And mercury poisoning, apparently."

She offered a weak smile. "Guess I'll be working some overnights then."

"That's ridiculous. You're being blackmailed."

"It's not that big of a deal. I'll go in tomorrow at 7 PM." Kali finished her small plate of food before standing up to clean the table.

"Please, let me do that," Craig said, trying to pick up the plates.

"No, it's alright," she said, pulling the pile of dishes in close. "I need something to do now so I can stay up late to get on schedule."

"Ah, right." He stepped towards her, plate in hand. "I'm very sorry to bring you all of this trouble."

"It's alright," she said, pulling out some plastic containers. "Would you like some of this food downstairs?"

"That'd be nice," he said. "You know, I can get a job, pay off my tab here and find another place to stay."

"Alright Craig," she replied, busying herself with the dishes.


Obviously she didn't think it was possible. Perhaps it wasn't. But he wanted to try, at least. He owed her that much.

"We could watch some movies tonight, then?" He suggested. "To get you on an overnight schedule?"

"No," Kali replied quickly. "I've got a lot of things I need to catch up on."

"Oh. Right."

He continued clearing the table. Kali focused on washing the dishes and packing up the food. Craig took the hint. He picked up his containers of food, thanked her again, and headed down to the basement.

Once downstairs, he sat with his head in his hands. Kali was some sort of living angel. She took in stray animals and people, even when she personally suffered for it.

Why couldn't he remember *anything* about his past life? Why was he such a drag on her? He decided it was time to get serious about finding out who he was. Plus, he needed to generate an income, so any investigation into Kali's behavior would show that she simply allowed him to rent a room. Nothing more.

Nothing more at all.

# Chapter 7

Despite Kali's efforts to stay up that night, her sleep schedule was poorly adjusted for her shift on Sunday. Luckily, it was somewhat quiet in the ICU. Her patient was relatively stable and she drank a lot of coffee to get through. When 7 AM hit, she gave her bedside report to the morning nurse and headed home. As soon as she got in the door, she went upstairs and passed out.

She awoke later that day around four in the afternoon, groggy and disoriented. Her stomach was upset with her for changing schedules, so she decided to skip breakfast and try tea first. She went downstairs to boil some water.

After a few minutes, she heard a knock on the door. Craig.

"Come in," she said.

"Morning sleepy head!" he replied, walking in excitedly. "I've been waiting all day for you to wake up."

She raised an eyebrow at him, but made no response. His black eye looked rough – it was dark and fully formed. She had a fleeting feeling of sadness and gratitude towards him. As afraid as she was that she would end up on the news as a missing person after letting a strange man into her rental, he actually protected her when the time came. And he took an elbow to the eye. It somehow made him look rugged and even more handsome. She brushed the thought away.

"Oh?" she said.

"Have you checked your phone yet?" he continued.

"No, why?" Was there more from Betsy?

"Oh," he said, voice falling slightly. "Nothing. I just – well, you'll see."

Slightly concerned what he could mean, Kali searched around for her phone. She opened the screen to see that she had five voicemails.

"Oh, I didn't notice that yesterday. Are these all from you?"

"The messages?" He waved a hand, "Yeah. I had a pretty exciting day while looking for a job. So whenever I saw an unattended phone, I called you to leave an update."

She felt her sternness starting to crack. "Unattended? Like payphones?"

"There aren't many of those around, if you can believe it. No, I mean phones in stores and things."

"I see," she said.

"Are you hungry?" he asked. "I had some terrific oatmeal at Mac-Donalds yesterday, so I bought a pack at the corner market. I'll make you some."

Hm. That actually sounded pretty good. Better than what she had in mind for breakfast, which was nothing. Also, did he say Mac-Donalds?

"Okay," she said.

He went downstairs to get the oatmeal. Why was he so excited to see her? It was kind of odd. Although, she was the only person he knew in the world. It sort of made sense.

She set down her tea and picked up her phone.

Message one. "Kali, it's Craig. Just wanted to let you know that I've picked up applications for work at this little bar downtown called Pubs. I suppose they wanted to be clear it was a pub? I'm not sure. I think my heritage may help here. More later."

Message two. "Hey, it's Craig. Hope your day is going well. Wanted to make sure I remembered to ask you, do you think anyone will notice if I make up a social security number? Thanks."

Kali shot him a look, but he was intently reading the directions on the package of the oatmeal. He'd located the microwave and apparently knew how to use it.

Message three. "It's me. I have good news and bad news. The good news is I was able to leave a report at the police station. The bad news is that I had to leave your phone number for updates."

"Craig!" she called out.

"What, too much water? Or would you prefer milk?"

"You left my phone number at the police station?"

"Oh, that," he said, leaning against the counter. "Well, yes. I don't have my own, do I?"

Kali glared at him. "Don't go all flippant and British on me," she said. "What if Betsy connects that and figures out that you're staying here?"

"Does Betsy moonlight at the police station? Don't worry about it!" he said, turning back to the microwave.

Kali sighed. It was a stretch, she knew. But she could take one tiny seed of irrational fear and let it grow into a monster that kept her awake all night. She was famous for it, in fact. Not that Craig would know that. Not that he *needed* to know.

Message four. "Kali honey, it's your mom. Just wanted to check in and see how you're doing! Dad and I are so proud of you taking on all this responsibility in your promotion. We miss you, please call when you have a chance and let us know how it's going. Love you!"

Oops. Kali usually called her mom every other day or so, but with her new tenant, she'd slipped up on her schedule. What was she going to tell her parents about this man living in the basement? They might be a bit concerned – but she should tell them. In case she *did* end up on the news.

Message five. "You'll never believe what I found!" She looked at her phone. That was the whole message: Craig whispering, "You'll never believe what I found!"


Craig came over and proudly set the oatmeal in front of her. "Here you are, it's not quite as good as what I had at Mac-Donalds, but I find the brown sugar to be quite good."

"Thanks," she replied, lifting the spoon. "And don't worry about competing with McDonalds. You can't beat them. They're too good."

He watched her expectantly. "What do you think?"

She took a bite. It was a bowl of slightly watery maple brown sugar oatmeal. Not exactly a revelation. "It's good, thank you."

"Good," he replied, satisfied.

"What was this last voicemail about? You found something?"

"Oh, right. It's a surprise. Downstairs. Let me get it."

Oh boy. What was this going to be? She tried to take another bite of the oatmeal but her stomach rumbled in protest.

Craig ascended the stairs slowly, then walked into the kitchen backwards. "Are you ready?" he asked, looking back at her.

She nodded. She was too tired to actually be ready for anything – she was so tired that it felt like her eyes were shrinking into her head.

He turned around, revealing a small gray and white kitten sitting in his hands. "Ta-da!"

"Oh my gosh!" Kali exclaimed, standing up instinctively to take the little guy into her arms. She delicately picked him up and he let out one small meow.

"I heard him meowing when I was walking around town," Craig said. "I found him under a car, I think he was trying to stay warm."

Kali turned the kitten to look into his round, clear eyes. "Did you find any other kittens nearby?"

"No," Craig said, crossing his arms. "Unfortunately not. I stuck him in my jacket to keep him warm and looked around for a good half hour, but there was nothing. I have no idea where he came from."

"Well don't you have *the cutest little white toes!*" Kali gushed, taking one white-tipped paw into the palm of her hand. She heard a laugh escape from Craig, which brought her back to reality. She was a little delirious and forgot herself.

She cleared her throat before saying, "I'll take him to the shelter to see if he has a microchip or if he belongs to someone. And to get a check up."

"Alright. Could they run the micro-chipper machine over me as well? To see if I belong to someone?"

Kali laughed and pulled the kitten in closer. "You can come if you want, but they're not going to scan you."

"What should we call him?"

"Oh, it's probably best not to get too attached." Kali adored her foster cats, but felt like it was irresponsible to have a cat of her own – she worried they'd get too lonely when she was working all those hours.

Craig was unfazed. "What was the name of the beast in *Beauty and the Beast*? Was it Gaston?"

Kali scowled at him. "He's not a beast! And no, Gaston was the name of the arrogant guy."

Craig reached for one of the kitten's white paws. "No, that doesn't suit him. I guess we'll have to stick with Beast then."

"He's too tiny to be called Beast!" Kali protested. "He's much more like...Chip. The little tea cup."

Craig smiled. "Chip it is then."

They headed out towards Kali's car, which was covered in two inches of snow. Kali asked Craig to hold onto the kitten so she could dust off the car, but he insisted that he would do it.

"No, really, it's fine," she said, trying to keep the snow brush out of his reach.

"I'm much more suited to the job," he replied, pulling the kitten from his jacket with one hand and reaching for the brush with the other. "I'm taller, I have longer arms, and I haven't done any work today so I have plenty of energy."

Normally she wouldn't give up that easily, but the first overnight left her extraordinarily tired. She released the brush and took the kitten into her own jacket.

"I'm going to sit in the car and make a call then," she said.

"Perfect!"

She settled into the driver's seat, turning the key in the ignition. It would take some time to warm up, but at least it wasn't windy inside the car. She pulled out her phone and dialed her mom's number.

"Hi honey!" her mom said brightly.

"Hi mom."

"How are you? What's new? Hows the ICU treating you?"

"Oh, it's pretty good," Kali said with a sigh. "Sorry I haven't been in touch, I got pulled into some surprise overnights for the next few days."

"Well that's a bummer," her mom said. "What time do you have to go into work today?"

"Seven, but right now I'm headed to the animal shelter."

"Oh really?"

"Yeah, I found a new kitten so I'm taking him to be checked out."

At that moment, Craig swiped the snow off of the windshield before attempting to scrape a smiley face in the ice beneath. Kali put her hand over her phone to muffle the noise.

"What's that sound?" her mom asked.

"Oh, it's someone scraping off a car." Technically true.

"Oh, gotcha."

They chatted for another few minutes before Craig finished his work and came back to sit down in the car. Kali pressed her finger to her lips to signal that he needed to be quiet. She hoped she'd have a chance to tell her mom about the strange man living in her basement apartment, but she didn't find the right moment. It'd have to wait until Craig wasn't around.

"Alright mom," she said, "I'm going to head out now, my car is all warmed up."

"Alright sweetie! Oh, one more thing. Did you hear that Steven had to fire two of his employees?"

"No, what happened?" Steven was her best friend Ashley's husband; he had his own business as a contractor. She hadn't had much time to catch up with Ashley since starting in the ICU either; they used to get lunch together because Ashley worked on the ortho-pedic floor as a nurse, but recently their schedules didn't align.

"Oh, they just weren't showing up to work. He's in a terrible bind. Can't find anyone to help him and he's got big jobs lined up!"

The idea hit Kali almost instantly. Of course. Why hadn't she thought of this before? "I actually might have someone who could help him."

"That would be lovely!" she said. "Alright, well I don't want you on the phone when you're driving, so you get going."

"Alright mom, love you."

"Love you too!"

She disconnected the call and pulled Chip out of her jacket to transfer to Craig.

"Now what is this I hear about you helping yet another person?" Craig asked, unzipping his jacket to accept the kitten.

"Not me," she said with a smile. "You."

# Chapter 8

Two days later, Craig was well into his first shift as a laborer when he decided that he was not impressed with the job. The first issue was that Steven put him on bathroom duty, despite Craig's suggestion that he could be handy with a paintbrush in the other room.

"No," Steven said. "You'll start with the toilet. Drain the water and get it out of the floor."

"Right," Craig said. "Out of the floor. Coming right up."

Craig had no idea how to do that. He hoped that some of this handy work knowledge would come to him easily, like setting the table did. No such luck. He stared at the toilet for a few minutes. It seemed entirely connected to the floor, as if the floor and the toilet were one. Perhaps they'd *always* been one. Whoever built the house put up walls, windows, and this toilet. Worst of all, it was filthy. He certainly didn't want to stick his hands in there to get the water out. In fact, it needed a good scrubbing before he would even consider getting near it.

Steven came back ten minutes later to find Craig on his hands and knees, scrubbing the toilet with gloved hands.

"Uh, how's it going?"

Craig turned around, surprised. "Oh, hey Steven."

"You want to tell me what you're doing?"

"Well," Craig said, raising himself up, "this toilet was filthy."

"Okay?"

"And before I got my hands in there, I wanted to make sure it was sanitary. Also, if the water spilled..." Craig shuddered.

Steven stared at him for a moment before responding. "Why didn't you just lift the lid of the tank?"

"Oh," Craig turned to look at the toilet. "Where is that?"

"Right here," Steven said, pointing. He lifted the lid to reveal the water inside.

"Well, that's brilliant. That would make a lot of sense. So we dump the water from there first, or...?"

"No. You can flush most of it, and the rest take out with this." Steven handed him a large, yellow sponge.

"Ah. Right. Sorry Steven, I don't know that I've ever done this before. And if I have, I don't remember."

"It's alright. I guess I should've thought of that. And use this to undo the bolts, then you can lift it right out of the floor."

Craig accepted another tool. "Oh, that's – okay, lovely."

Once he had the instructions, it didn't take long for Craig to accomplish the task. He still found the toilet to be gross. He thought throwing it out and starting over may be the best option for these people. Even grosser was the large, dark pipe that lived under the toilet, now exposed for everyone to see. Craig thought the pipe could use some bleach, perhaps a gallon or so, but he didn't have the chance to do that.

Once Steven saw Craig carry the toilet out of the bathroom, he handed him a mallet and a wedge sort of thing. He said he needed to use it to pull up the tiles.

"As in – break them? And totally remove them?"

"Yes. Totally demo it."

"Demo, right."

The bathroom was rather large and unfortunately, so were the tiles. It took him an hour and a half of kneeling to break up and rip them out of the floor. His knees and his back were killing him by the end. Each time he finished a task, Steven would appear and assign him an even more unpleasant one. Pull up the subfloor. Put down new subfloor. Bend over to do everything.

Of those first six hours, Craig spent most of them hunched over. If Kali weren't at work, he'd call her and ask her to come pick him up. He could cite creative differences with Steven.

Steven seemed to think that everything needed to be done at once, one thing after the other. Craig thought there should be ample time for breaks. Perhaps even naps. Unfortunately, Craig wasn't in charge, so he kept working. The only breaks Craig took were to eat. First, he had the ever-so-sweetly packed lunch that Kali made him.

"I'm making my own, so I'll just throw one together for you, too," she'd told him that morning. "Nothing special. I hope you like sad, single people food like hard boiled eggs and yogurt."

"My favorite," he'd replied with a smile.

It seemed like she always needed to make it clear to him that she wasn't being nice to him *on purpose*, but instead it was just convenient for her. But Craig saw through it. Kali was the kind of person who couldn't stand not helping others. She gave her whole heart to the world around her. No wonder she was such a terrific nurse. And a terrific person in general.

Craig tried to refocus his thoughts as he slowly chewed the turkey sandwich she made him, but he found it impossible. Of all the people he knew in the world right now, and admittedly he didn't know many, Kali was his absolute favorite. What a wonder it would be to make her list of top 10, or even top 20 people.

Even the lunch she packed was full of love. Craig didn't flatter himself that she had any feelings for him, but it was interesting that it was almost as though she didn't know any other way to treat people. His heavy lunch bag contained three hard boiled eggs, a turkey sandwich, a container of yogurt, a bag of pretzels, plus a banana and an apple.

"You're a – large man," she'd said. "I imagine you need to eat a lot."

He'd laughed at her then, but after working so many hours on the floor, he greatly appreciated his giant lunch.

He went back to work, a little stiffer than before, but completely full. They put in a total of twelve hours that day. Craig thought it would never end. He was relieved when Steven finally said it was time to pack up and go home.

"You're slow," Steven commented, giving Craig a ginger pat on the back, "but at least you're steady."

"Thanks Steven," Craig replied. "You're terrible at explaining things, but at least you were enough of a sucker to take me on today."

Steven let out a hearty laugh "You're welcome."

Craig got home and took a hot shower. Though he initially intended to stretch his legs and back, he felt rather relaxed after the shower and decided to take a seat on the couch. He told himself he'd sit for just a few minutes, but as soon as he sat down, he practically melted into the cushion. It was so comfortable that he could hardly trouble himself to lean forward and grab the TV remote. He put on a cooking show and dozed off immediately.

He awoke early in the morning when he heard Kali come into the house. Excited by the prospect of seeing her, he hopped off of the couch and gently knocked on the door separating their living spaces.

He paused for a moment to listen for her usual annoyed sigh, but heard nothing. He knocked a bit louder, then listened again.

Almost pressing his ear to the door, Craig thought he could make out a noise – but no, it couldn't be. It sounded like someone crying. Did something happen to Kali? One of her cats? Without thinking, he tried the door handle, and surprisingly, it turned.

He quietly opened the door and peaked his head in. There was only one light on, and in the darkness he could make out Kali's small figure huddled on the couch. She was sobbing.

"Kali, are you okay?" he called from the doorway.

"Yes, I'm – " She made some sort of a hiccup-sob hybrid noise, then started crying again.

Craig rushed over to her. There was nothing more he'd like to do than scoop her up in his arms and comfort her – but he realized that was probably inappropriate. He settled for sitting down beside her.

"What's going on?' he said gently. He saw a box of tissues in the far corner and fetched them for her.

She accepted a tissue and blew her nose. "Thanks."

"Here," he said, handing her two more and accepting the snotty tissue in return.

She wiped her eyes and took a deep breath. "My patient died."

"Oh," Craig replied. That was a bit awkward. His initial thought was to make a joke, but he couldn't think of a single thing that wouldn't be horrible to say. "I'm sorry."

Kali pinched her lips and nodded. "Yeah, me too."

They sat in silence for a moment. Craig hated silence.

"Was it that toad Betsy's fault?"

Kali laughed.

Good – at least Betsy was always a safe target.

"No," she replied. "He had an accident."

"You mean Betsy dropped him on the floor?"

"No," Kali smiled. "Nothing like that. He had – he came in after a car accident."

Craig frowned. "Oh."

"And the last few days, I've been taking care of him. He was just a kid...and his parents were finally able to make it in today, because they live halfway across the country..." she broke down into sobs again.

Craig felt his jaw tighten. He hated to see her so upset. He wished he could bring the kid back from the dead. Something. Anything. He handed her another tissue. She looked so small and alone sitting there on the couch, all curled up. He couldn't stop himself – he inched closer to her and put an arm around her shoulder.

She didn't snuggle into him or anything, but she didn't push him away either.

"It sounds like there was nothing you could have done differently," he said softly.

Kali shook her head. "He was only twenty...same as my little brother. And to see his parents come in, and they just – " She stopped talking and closed her eyes.

"It's okay," Craig said.

She started crying again, more quietly than before, and leaned into him. He wrapped his other arm around her and held her as she sobbed. He decided it was best to say nothing.

After a while, Kali stopped crying and seemed to only be sniffling. Craig suggested that she go upstairs, take a shower, and go to bed. She nodded and went upstairs without saying another word.

Craig stared at the dark hallway where she'd disappeared. He had about thirty minutes before Steven would be there to pick him up. Initially, he'd planned to tell Steven thanks, but no thanks – that he couldn't stomach another day on the job. But now...

Not only had he gotten Kali in trouble at work, then he decided that he'd quit the job she got him because he was sore. And lazy. Craig felt ashamed of himself. How could he be such a baby when Kali's job was so much harder?

He straightened out, joints and back making concerning popping noises, found Kali's lunch bag and washed the containers. He refilled them with what he thought she'd had in her lunch before – carrots, hummus. He made her a turkey sandwich, and since he didn't know how to hard boil eggs, he threw in a baggie of little chocolates he'd found in the pantry. After setting her pink lunch box in the fridge, he wrote a quick note to make sure she didn't miss it.

He threw together his own lunch as well, making a mental note that he needed to pick up the next grocery bill after he was paid.

Craig went outside, watching his breath in the cold morning air as he waited for Steven to arrive. Luckily, Steven was a punctual man and Craig only had to wait about five minutes.

"Morning Craig."

"Morning Steven," Craig said, settling into the passenger seat of the truck.

"I was afraid you might not show up today," Steven said with a smirk.

Craig laughed. His whole body ached. But the little pit of shame that burned in his stomach was worse than being sore. "How could you ever doubt me?"

# Chapter 9

By the end of her string of overnights in the ICU, Kali was exhausted. She tried to reset her sleep schedule on Thursday by staying up until 2 PM and then taking a short nap. It sort of worked, but she still felt a bit delirious. And a little itchy.

It didn't take long for her to realize that the itchiness was from flea bites. Craig's rescue kitten Chip, as adorable as he was, came with some unwanted guests. Normally, Kali would've noticed fleas immediately, but she simply wasn't herself that week. The sleep deprivation and the loss of her twenty year old patient left her in a bit of a daze. Nothing was a better example of that than the fact that she broke down in front of Craig. Kali never broke down in front of anyone. Not anymore, at least. And she *definitely* never cried in anyone's arms. That was really something new for her. Yet his strong arms were really quite nice...

She snapped herself out of it. There was no need to think about Craig's strong arms. His arms were for ripping up kitchens and bathrooms and stuff. At least that was the message she got through her best friend Ashley – apparently Craig was quite the help on the job. His amnesia caused some issues, sure, but overall he'd put in a lot of hours and Steven couldn't be happier.

Ashley not only heard things through Steven, she also saw for herself when she stopped by on her day off to bring lunch for the guys. She was just *tickled* to meet Craig.

"Kali," she'd texted immediately, "why didn't you tell me that Craig looks like he belongs on a magazine cover?"

"I didn't think it was relevant," Kali responded. There was no point denying that he was attractive, but she didn't have to gush like a schoolgirl.

Ashley wasn't convinced. "It's always relevant. And here I thought you were hosting some sixty year old man, not a swimsuit model!"

Swimsuit model? Kali found it odd that Ashley was imagining Craig in his swimsuit. Or maybe she saw him with his shirt off. It didn't matter – Kali's relationship with Craig was strictly professional. She didn't date patients – she didn't date at all, in fact. Ashley knew that. She hadn't been on a date since her fiancé died when they were both 19. There was that one time that Ashley tricked her into a double date, but that didn't count because Kali went home as soon as politeness allowed.

Kali knew it was only a matter of time before Ashley blabbed to her family that she had a "swimsuit model" staying in her rental. It was perfect timing, then, that Kali was going home for her brother's birthday that weekend. She could tell her parents about Craig, they could meet him, and they both needed a place to stay while her townhouse was sprayed for fleas.

It was still a bit awkward to bring it up.

Kali started with, "It's kind of an odd situation, mom."

"Why is that?"

"Well – he was my patient in the ICU. Just for a day. And then later, I found him at the food bank. He had nowhere to stay, so I let him stay in the basement. But now he's working with Steven, so – "

"Oh honey, that's such a kind thing for you to do!"

Her mom didn't seem fazed *at all*. Kali explained the amnesia, which her mom found fascinating.

"Of course you can bring him!" she'd said, almost a bit too quickly. "We'd love to have him!"

"Thanks, mom. See you Saturday!"

Kali couldn't tell if it was her mom's friendly midwestern hospitality coming out, or if Ashley told her how attractive Craig was. She decided not to dwell on it.

On the drive up, Craig asked nearly a hundred questions about her family. Kali was somewhat amused by how interested he was.

"So your dad – he still runs the paper mill?"

"No – he did when we were growing up. But it burned down when I was fifteen."

Craig cringed. "Best not to bring that up, huh?"

"No," Kali laughed. "It's okay. We were all devastated at the time, of course, but it ended up being a blessing in disguise."

"Is this your confession that you set the fire, then?"

"No," Kali replied, keeping her eyes on the road, even though she wanted to shoot him a dirty look. "That's not what I'm saying. It was just that the business wasn't doing great, and after that, a lot of the mills closed down anyway."

"Ah, I see."

"And when my dad got the insurance money – "

Craig interrupted her, "Was this before or after you hid all the evidence of your involvement in the mill's demise?"

"They did an investigation and found out that it was caused by a lightning strike!"

"You're kidding!" Craig exclaimed. "I did not see that coming! You used some sort of witchcraft to call the lightning?"

Kali continued, ignoring him. "After he got the insurance money, he wanted to open up another mill. But my mom wouldn't let him – she knew that we'd be bankrupt within five years."

"And you'd have to go back to working the carnival booth, wasting your magical powers on guessing people's weights again."

She turned to him for a moment to give him a stern look. He smiled broadly. It was easier to just go along with his nonsense at this point. "Exactly. You figured me out. So my mom convinced him to build a daycare instead."

"Oh, that's quite different than a paper mill."

Kali nodded. "She'd always wanted to run one and it was the perfect opportunity. Plus, when a lot of the other mills closed down and people were looking for work, we were able to watch their kids for cheap. Or let's be honest, most of the time it was free."

"That seems like a poor business strategy," Craig replied.

"Well – yeah. But we got by. And we helped the people in our community get by, too."

"Ah," Craig said with a smile. "I now see where you get your martyrdom."

"Yeah." Kali frowned. She wondered if Craig came from a family that didn't think it was important to help others. It certainly seemed like it. Then again, he had no memory of his old life. Perhaps he ran with a crowd of other beautiful, swimsuit model people who spent their free time admiring themselves in mirrors. She reminded herself that he probably had a beautiful wife in that old life – someone who may be frantically looking for him. Not frantically enough, apparently. A laugh popped out of her mouth.

"What's so funny?" he asked.

"Oh, nothing. Are you sure you don't want to post your picture online somewhere so your family can find you?"

"Absolutely not," he said firmly. "One day when you were at work, I watched that movie *Overboard*."

"Never saw it," she replied.

"In it, Goldie Hawn falls off a boat, ends up with amnesia. Not unlike yours truly. And a guy who has a grudge against her shows up pretending to be her husband. Brings doctored photos and everything."

"Wait I have seen this," she said. "You're afraid that a man will show up to claim you and you'll fall in love with him?"

"Precisely." He dropped his voice, "And I don't think it's a stretch to think that someone might hold a grudge against me."

"Fair point," she conceded.

By the time they arrived at her parents' house, Craig knew most of the history of each member of her family. It was a bit odd that he was so inquisitive, but she also wondered how well he'd remember what she told him. Maybe he had some short term memory loss as well. She made note of it – he needed to follow up with a neurologist if his memory didn't return soon.

Kali pulled into the driveway and before she even put the car in park, her mom ran out of the house waving manically.

"Welcome home sweetie!" she said, tapping on the driver's window.

Craig waved back. "Haven't been home in some time, eh?" he asked Kali.

"I was home three weeks ago," she replied in a low voice. She opened the door and gave her mom a tight hug.

"Hey mom, how are you?"

"I am so happy to have all my babies under one roof this week-end!" She turned, arms open, towards Craig. "And you must be Craig! I've heard so much about you!"

Craig accepted her hug. "Not from Kali, I'm sure?"

"No," Kali said flatly. "You don't have to be so nice to him, mom. He's not the king of England."

"Or am I?" Craig said with a mischievous smile.

"Maybe the king of fleas!" Kali called over her shoulder, walking into the house. Her mom was *way* too excited to meet him, and she suspected that Ashley had something to do with it.

"Thank you for having me, Mrs. Mitchell."

"Oh please, call me Candice!"


Kali rolled her eyes. This was going to be a long weekend.

# Chapter 10

They walked into the house and were immediately greeted by a small, wiry dog. Craig kneeled down to pet him and was promptly knocked over when a larger black Labrador came bounding out of the kitchen.

"Nice to meet you too!" Craig said through laughter.

"Cookie!" Candice exclaimed, exasperated. "That is *not* polite!" She pulled the dog off of Craig, allowing him to stand up.

"Sorry, it was my mistake, making myself a target like that." He stood and dusted some of the dog hair off of his jeans.

"Don't let them push you around," Candice said. "Especially if they try to knock you off of the couch tonight. Oh, I'm making up the couch for your bed, I hope that's alright?"

"Sure, that sounds perfect."

"You can just leave your bag here for now. Marcy! Ella! Your sister is home!" She went into the kitchen to address a timer that was going off.

Two girls with the same striking dark hair as Kali emerged at the top of the stairs. They froze when they saw Craig.

"Hello," he said with a small wave.

The one with the shorter hair and heavy eye liner descended the stairs first. "Hi, I'm Marcy."

"Ah yes, the musician of the family. It's nice to meet you, I'm Craig." He extended his hand and she accepted it with a blush.

The second girl followed and extended her hand. "Hi."

"Hello – Ella, right?" Craig said, shaking her hand.

She nodded. "That's right, the *brains* of the family."

Kali snickered. "When did you come up with that Ella?"

"When I got a 4.0 last semester!"

Marcy crossed her arms. "Didn't you get a B in art?"

Ella shrugged. "They don't count that when you're applying to college. Art isn't a real subject."

"Yes they do," Marcy protested, "all of the classes count!"

"Even *music?* That seems dumb," Ella said.


Candice popped her head out of the kitchen. "Girls, no fighting on your brother's birthday!"

"Yeah," said the man who just strolled into the living room. "Save it for your own birthday!"

"Hi dad," Kali said, giving him a hug. "This is Craig, my first tenant."

Craig felt nervous, but he wasn't sure why. He quickly stuck out his hand for a handshake. Kali's dad looked down at it, then back at Craig, hands still in his pockets.

"So you're the man living in my daughter's basement, rent free?"

Craig swallowed hard, almost like a cartoon character. Kali failed to mention that her dad was as stern as she was. "That's right, sir, but very soon I hope to – "

He roared with laughter, pulling Craig into a hug before he could finish talking. "I'm just messing with you, kiddo." He patted him roughly on the back. "I'm Fred, welcome to The House of Mitchell."

"Hi Fred, great to meet you," Craig said, still a bit startled by it all.

"Don't mind the twins," Fred continued. "They're just mad that we make them share their birthday every year. And their room. And their identity – we only registered one of them when they were born, so now they have to alternate who gets to go to school every day."

This time Craig was ready for the joke and responded with a laugh.

"Dad," Kali said, rubbing her forehead, "Don't you think it's time to retire that joke?"

"No!" He shook his head. "Every time I meet someone new, I get to use it. That's the rule. Right girls?"

Ella and Marcy almost simultaneously rolled their eyes. It was like the teenager olympics of eye rolling. Craig tried to suppress a smile. Kali's family was everything he hoped they'd be and more.

"Craig," Marcy stepped forward. "Let me take you on a tour of the house."

"Sure, sounds lovely."

There wasn't much to tour; the house had three rather tight bedrooms, one bathroom, and a finished basement.

"This was my brother's room before he went to college," Marcy said of the basement, "but now I'm pretty much exclusively using it as my studio."

"Ah, very nice," Craig replied, looking around admiringly.

"Would you like to hear a song?" she asked, picking up her guitar.

Ella appeared in the doorway. "I'm sure he didn't come all this way to listen to you play."

Craig smiled. "That'd be nice."

Marcy didn't miss a beat. "What kind of music do you like? British stuff? I know a lot of British rock," she said confidently.

"Well, to be honest – I don't remember much of what music I like."

"Oh, right. The amnesia." She nodded. "Mom told me about that."

"I'm sure I'll like anything you play."

Marcy brightened. "Alright, tell me if you know this one."

She started into a rather unpleasant sounding string of notes, followed by some low, melancholy lyrics. It went on for what Craig thought may have been an hour or two, but it was likely only a few minutes. He forced himself to nod intently.

When she hit the last note, he clapped and said, "Bravo!"

"Did you recognize it?" she asked.

He frowned. "I can't say that I did, but that's not personal, I assure you. I don't even know my own last name."

"But you thought you could have heard it, like, on the radio?"

It slowly dawned on him what she was getting at. "Yes," he said quickly, "definitely."

Ella let out a loud sigh from the doorway.

"See," Marcy said. "I *told* you it was good enough to be on the radio."

There was some commotion upstairs and Candice yelled that "the birthday boy" arrived and that they needed to come and help set the table. Craig followed them upstairs, and after saying a brief hello to Kali's brother Cody, he spent a painful few minutes hovering around the kitchen. He wanted to help with something, but ended up just being a nuisance as Candice tried to check some things on the stove and the girls went back and forth to grab things for the table.

Unable to figure out how to help, he removed himself from the kitchen and instead decided to talk to Cody.

"Long drive in?" he asked.

"No, not too bad. I go to school in Milwaukee."

"Ah," Craig said, pretending he knew where Milwaukee was in relation to Madison. "Do you like it there?"

"Yeah, so far so good."

"And you're studying...?"

"Engineering," Cody said with a shrug. "It's alright. A lot of math. How long have you and Kali been together?"

Craig scratched his head and laughed. Clearly Cody was not as up to date on Kali's life as her twin sisters were. Probably a function of living away from home – and of being a guy.

Kali stepped in and gave Cody a hug. "Hey bro, happy birthday." She looked at Craig. "He's not my boyfriend. He's my... tenant."

"Oh!" Cody said. "Sorry. It's just my sister hasn't had a boyfriend since – well, since Luke."

"Ooh," Craig cooed, turning toward Kali. "*Luke* was it?"

Kali's face turned red. Without saying a word, she immediately left the room.

Craig had the urge to go after her, but Cody started talking again. "Uh – sorry. I assumed you knew."

Craig lowered his voice. "Knew what?"

"About her fiancé."

Craig shook his head. "She never mentioned it."

"Oh. Well – she – maybe you should just ask her later."

"Alright."

At that moment, Candice shooed everyone towards the dining room. "We're going to have cake first," she said. "Just the way you like it Cody!"

They all made their way to the table, Craig feeling exceptionally awkward and bad. He was about to get up and find Kali when she appeared at the end of the table.

"Is everything okay?" Craig asked quietly. She looked totally recovered – perhaps he'd imagined that she was upset.

"Yeah, why?" she gave him a puzzled look. She was a good actress, but she wasn't that good. Craig could tell she was hiding something. Whatever it was, she wasn't going to discuss it in front of everyone. He decided to drop it.

Candice came in carrying a large, homemade cake that was wonderfully on fire with twenty candles. They sang happy birthday, cut the cake, and then Cody opened a few presents. The twins got him a hooded sweatshirt; Kali got him a new tablet to use for school.

Craig felt a bit sheepish for not bringing anything. He was supposed to be paid at the end of his second week, so he was still technically broke. He didn't get a chance to delve too deeply into his embarrassment, though, because Marcy thought of a fun game to play before dinner was served.

"Alright, so we're going to do a word association game. I'm going to say a word, and you'll say the first thing that comes to your mind. It might help unbury some of your memories!"

It seemed like a decent idea to Craig. "Okay."

"Alright, are you ready? No thinking, just say what comes into your head."

"Got it."

"Okay – city!"

Craig paused. "Landscape?"

She waved a hand. "That took too long. Just say what comes into your head."

"Right, sorry." He leaned forward to improve his focus.

"It's okay," Marcy said. "Ready? Food!"

He didn't hesitate this time. "Pancakes."

The table erupted into laughter. He looked around. "What's so funny?"

"You just said that really seriously," Kali said. "Have you even had pancakes before?"

"Well, not that I know of," responded Craig. "But I saw an advertisement for them on TV and I thought they looked quite good."

More laughter. Ella decided she wanted to get in on the fun. "Let me ask some! Craig, look at me. Focus, okay?"

He tried to stop smiling and look at her. "Ready."

"Car!"

"Driver."

"House!"

"Home."

"Mom!"

"Maggie."

Ella paused for a moment and narrowed her eyes. "Is that your mom's name?"

Craig stopped for a moment. "It is. My mum's name is Maggie!"

"It worked!" Marcy said triumphantly.

"Craig," Kali said, staring at him, "What's her last name?"

He looked down, trying to refocus. Nothing came to him. "I don't know," he said finally.

"That's okay," Marcy said, hands clasped. "We're getting somewhere."

The questioning went on for another twenty minutes, everyone taking turns with asking. Craig didn't have any more revelations. He was a bit distracted, actually, thinking the name Maggie over and over again. He hoped he could see his mother's face, or catch some other detail about her. The harder he tried, the further away it seemed.

Dinner was served not too long after the game started to lose its luster. Candice made Cody's favorite meal, some sort of a pot roast that Craig thought was delicious. After dinner, Craig helped clear the table, and then everyone went into the living room to play Pictionary.

It took a few minutes to explain the rules to Craig, but once he figured it out, he felt rather competitive. Unfortunately, every other member of the family was better at the game than he was, and he discovered that he was also terrible at drawing pictures.

At one point, Fred held up Craig's sad drawing of a classroom and said, "Craig, I think you're going to need to bring this to your doctor."

"What! It's clearly a classroom."

"Why did you make all of these little tombstones..." Fred said, pointing. "I think a psychiatrist needs to take a look at this."

"Those are desks," Craig insisted.

Kali agreed. "I'll make sure it gets in his file."

Craig laughed so hard that night that his face hurt. He was exhausted by the time everyone went to bed for the night and he settled onto the couch. It was so comically small that he either had to have his legs stick off a few feet or curl up like a small dog. It didn't bother him, though. For some reason, these people welcomed him like he was a member of the family, not like the bizarre house guest that he was.

He closed his eyes. All he could see was Kali's laughing face. No matter what he tried to think about – his mother's name, his job, where he came from – all he could think of was Kali. Part of him wished that he'd never remember who he was. Maybe he could rent the basement from Kali for the rest of his life. That wouldn't be so bad.

He felt guilty, though. Surely he had people who cared about him – people who were looking for him. What if he had a girlfriend? A wife? And he was off falling in love with another woman?

Surely he'd remember if he were in love with someone else. No – Craig was sure that the only woman in his heart was Kali. Seeing her with her family only made him feel more mad in his adoration of her. There was no denying it.

He decided it was at least worth finding out who he was so he could then offer Kali the full truth. Perhaps it'd even tempt her into accepting him. He drifted into sleep, her face weaving in and out of his dreams.

# Chapter 11

Her mom made an embarrassing show of saying goodbye on Sunday and telling Craig that he was "always welcome to visit." Even her dad, who rarely commented on anything seriously, told Craig that it was "nice to have someone else with a sense of humor" around. Kali tried not to roll her eyes. Later, on the ride home, she told Craig that he must have children in his real life.

"Really?" He seemed a bit stunned. "I didn't even think of that."

"I'm just saying because you seem to have Dad Jokes pretty much down."

Craig smiled. "Oh."

Kali felt bad – he seemed lost in thought after her comment. She didn't mean to suggest that he *actually* had children, who he'd subsequently abandoned during his amnesia. Kali decided to leave the jokes to him.

He spoke up after a few minutes. "Your family – "

"Is nuts?" she said, cutting him off.

He shook his head. "I was going to say lovely."

"Ha, thanks," she replied. She wasn't used to serious Craig. "Well – that's nice of you to say."

"I wonder if I have a family. And if they're looking for me."

She offered him a pained smile. "I'm sure they are. You remembered your mom's name, that was good!"

"Yeah," he brightened a bit. "Thanks to Marcy."

They rode in silence for a few more minutes before Craig spoke again.

"I want to apologize for asking about Luke."

"It's okay, you didn't know." She had time to process it now, too. She was just surprised when Cody brought it up. "His birthday is coming up. In two weeks."

"Yeah?"

She nodded, keeping her eyes straight on the road. "I always take a day off. I visit his parents, and I visit his grave."

Craig looked at her but said nothing.

"We were high school sweethearts," she continued. "And in our last year of school, he found out he had cancer. Leukemia."

"How terrible," Craig said quietly.

Kali swallowed. It was terrible. She didn't know why she was telling him all of this. "He proposed to me – he made me promise we'd get married as soon as he beat the cancer. But he never did."

Craig turned to her. "Kali, I'm so sorry."

"It's okay," she said. "It was a long time ago." She avoided looking at him – she didn't want him to see the tears in her eyes. It *was* a long time ago, but Luke was the only man she'd ever loved. He was the only man she ever *would* love. That much she knew. There was no room for anyone else in her heart.

They arrived home shortly afterwards. Kali busied herself with running errands – bringing the animals over from her neighbor's house, running to the grocery store, packing lunches. Craig insisted on helping her as much as he could, but she only allowed him to help her with lunches. She wanted some time away from him. She was afraid he'd ask more about Luke – rather, she was afraid she'd blab more about Luke. It'd been so long since he passed away that no one asked about him anymore...even though she was always thinking of him.

Craig didn't bring it up again. Instead he asked her how to hard boil eggs; apparently, he felt guilty he wasn't able to pack her a decent lunch the other day. Kali thought it was more than decent – it'd been *years* since someone else packed a lunch for her. Somehow it always tasted better when someone else made it for you. She didn't tell him that, though; instead, she showed him the egg timer.

That evening, they watched *Casino Royale* on TV. Somehow, Craig knew not only the name of every Bond actor in the last fifteen years, he also knew the plots of all of the movies.

"Clearly, Bond is stored in a different part of my brain than all of my friends, family and loved ones."

"You must love him very much," Kali said with a smirk.

"I do," he replied, mockingly placing a hand over his heart.

They stayed up a bit too late that night because Craig insisted that she see the ending of the movie. Craig also made Kali promise that they would watch some of his other favorites that week. She agreed, if only because she hoped those memories were tied to something else in his life.

On Monday, they each returned to work and fell into a sort of routine where every evening, they'd sit down and watch a Bond movie. Craig was thrilled. Kali would never admit it, but she was happy to see him happy.

By the end of the week, Kali was wiped out. Betsy asked her to pick up an extra shift, and though she didn't say anything about Craig, Kali felt it was still implied that she was holding that over her head. How long could she do that, though? She'd have to find something new to bully her with eventually.

That Friday night, she and Craig settled onto the couch, as was their new routine.

"Alright, so do you want to watch *Tomorrow Never Dies?* Or do you want to pick something?"

Kali shrugged. "Whatever."

"I feel like I've been quite the movie hog," Craig said. "I'd like you to pick. I'm finished picking."

"It really doesn't matter to me. I will probably fall asleep in a few minutes anyway."

Craig frowned. "Right. Well, rest up for tomorrow."

"Why?"

"I have a surprise!"

"Oh no," Kali groaned.

"Oh, come now. You're going to like it," he said.

"What is it?"

"Well," he straightened up. "First of all, Steven paid me today. To be honest, I didn't think he would pull through, but he did."

"Uh huh," Kali said, too tired to tease him about his lack of faith in Steven.

"So that's the first good news. I can pay my rent for the last two weeks, and I can pick up the next grocery bill. And pay you back for the clothing."

Kali sighed. "That would probably take most of your first paycheck, and I don't need the money. It can wait a few weeks."

Craig crossed his arms. "I am good for it, you know."

She laughed. "I'm sure you are. I'm just saying, it's totally fair for you to have the full month to pay me."

"Fine. 'Til the end of the month, then."

"Deal," she said, closing her eyes. The couch was so comfortable that she couldn't resist.

"That may be better then, so I have enough to pay for dinner tomorrow."

Kali opened her eyes. "Where are you going?"

"*We* are going to Amalfi Corner."

"Are you serious?" Kali sat up. Her coworkers talked about that place all the time – it was *the* place to go for anniversaries and celebrations. Kali had never been, of course, because why would she spend all of that money on a fancy dinner just for herself?

"Oh, so you've heard of it?" Craig said, brightening. "That's good. I saw it one day when I went downtown on the bus and – "

"Craig, that place is really expensive. And you need a reservation like a month ahead of time."

He shrugged. "Well it's a good thing that I made a reservation the first time I walked by, isn't it?"

Her jaw dropped. "You're not serious."

"I am. And don't worry about the money, I just got paid and rent isn't due for another two weeks." He winked at her.

Kali laughed and shook her head. "I'm not going."

"It's my treat. Please. Let me do one nice thing for you in return for all the nice things you've done for me."

Kali sighed. What if Betsy saw her out? Then again, what were the chances that Betsy would be at the same restaurant that night? She didn't have anyone to go to dinner with either, that was for sure.

"Otherwise," Craig said, dropping his voice, "I'll have to ask your dad to go with me and I don't think he'd appreciate the ambiance."

"No, I don't think he would," she said. She bit her lip. What was the harm? It might be her only chance to go there for the foreseeable future. It's not like she had any plans that weekend, either.

"Alright," she finally said. "But I pay for myself. We go dutch."

"We have to dress up as Dutchmen? I can't stand for that," Craig said with the wave of a hand.

"It's a saying," she replied, "it means – "

"Is it?" he stood up abruptly. "Never heard of it. Would you like some popcorn?"

Kali didn't make it through much of the movie – she fell asleep about twenty minutes later and only awoke when Craig stood to turn off the TV around midnight. She sluggishly went upstairs and got ready for bed before falling asleep again.

The next morning, she got up early to run some errands around town. At one point, she considered popping into a store to find a new dress for dinner. It had been ages since she even thought about buying something pretty – she wasn't even sure if she had anything in her closet that would fit! She didn't want Craig to get the wrong idea, though. They were only going as friends. Also, it would be wasteful to buy a dress just to go out for one night. She didn't get out much, so she may never be able to wear it again.

Once she got home, she pulled her phone out of her bag to see that she'd gotten a text from Ashley.

"Hey Chica," it read, "I haven't seen you in forever. Want to come over for a girl's night? I bought clay face masks!"

Kali smiled. That would be nice – she felt guilty that she hadn't made more of an effort to see Ashley recently. "Sure, I'd love that! Craig is taking me to dinner at 6 tonight, though, as a thank you, so would it be too late if I came after that?"

Her reply came quickly. Too quickly. "Oh la la, a hot date! Don't let me interrupt!"

Kali sighed. "No. It's not that at all. I'll come over after?"

"Sure! See you then!"

There was a decent looking dress that Kali forgot she had in her closet. She felt a bit giddy as she got ready that night. It had been ages since she dressed up or went out for fun. Even for her birthday she tended to keep things low key; and though she very well could have gone to a nice restaurant like this with Ashley or her mom, that always seemed a bit lame to suggest. It really highlighted that she was alone in the world. Even if it were true, she didn't like to dwell on it.

Craig was waiting for her when she came down the stairs.

"Ready to go?" she asked.

He stood, mouth slightly open. "You look beautiful," he said.

Kali narrowed her eyes. "I feel like I should make it clear that we're going as friends?"

He cleared his throat. "Yes, of course. I know. Sorry."

She pulled on her coat. "Good." He stared at her for a moment more before he went to put on his own coat. He didn't look so bad himself.

Steven gave him a ride to pick up some more clothes that week. Naturally, everything he bought fit him perfectly and made him look even more like a model.

Ashley would've been so delighted if she saw him. Kali made a mental note to be sure that Ashley didn't get the chance – because then it would only be a matter of time before she gave Kali's mom a full report of how he looked. Kali wasn't interested in whatever scheme they were cooking up. Craig was just a friend – a tenant, actually – no matter how cute he was.

# Chapter 12

It was snowing, which made the drive a bit slow, but the walk to the restaurant was quite pretty. They arrived right on time but still had to wait ten minutes to be seated. Craig didn't mind – it's not like he had anywhere else to be. Spending time with Kali was his favorite thing to do. And tonight she looked so stunning that he could hardly stop himself from staring at her.

She'd insisted that they were going only as friends, but to the untrained eye, they looked like any other couple out on a date. The major difference, Craig noted, was that they talked a lot more than the actual couples; it seemed a handful of the restaurant patrons were sitting at tables, looking at their phones or at the ground, anywhere but at each other. How odd.

The restaurant was small and they were eventually seated at a table in the corner. Kali pored over the menu, unable to narrow down her choices.

"I can't decide if I want the fusilli or the gnocchi," she said.

"They serve gnocchi in a bread bowl," Craig observed. "That seems interesting."

"It does..." Kali was lost in thought.

"How about you get the gnocchi, I'll get the fusilli and that way you can try both?"

Kali smiled. "Okay!"

He leaned in. "Shall we give the calamari a go?"

"As an appetizer?" Kali frowned. "Is that octopus?"

"Squid, I believe. It's fried, so it should be unrecognizable."

"Alright, sure," she said, closing the menu. "I think we're ready."

She set the menu down and the waiter stopped by, took their order and dropped off a basket of bread. It was still warm from the oven.

"I could just die right now," Kali said, taking a bite of the bread. "This is *so good!*"

"Alright," Craig said, grabbing the bread basket from the table. "I wanted you to be happy, but not *that* happy. Can't have you dying, your mother would kill me."

Kali laughed heartily, covering her mouth. "Sorry," she said, "can I please have that back?"

"What," Craig said, holding the basket slightly above the table, "this? No, I'm sorry, it's been recalled by the kitchen staff."

"Why?"

"They're taking it to the homeless shelter later, actually, stop being so selfish."

"Oh, alright," Kali replied. She giggled.

Craig just about died himself. He'd never heard her giggle before. It didn't seem like a serious Kali thing to do – but he very much liked playful Kali.

"But listen, they don't know we still have ours," he said in a low voice. "So if fresh bread is what makes you happy, I'm willing to hide it from them so you can have the rest."

Kali raised her eyebrows. "Thanks Craig. Or should I say – Bond?"

He placed the basket back on the table and waved a hand. "Don't thank me. Thank my Queen for training me to be this clever."

Kali, who was taking a sip of water, choked out a laugh. "Will do," she said, once she regained her composure.

The appetizer arrived shortly after Kali finished off most of the bread. She picked up a piece of calamari and eyed it suspiciously. Craig popped one into his mouth and nodded. "Yep, just like I remember it."

Kali narrowed her eyes. "Of all things, do you really remember calamari?"

"No," he said, popping another into his mouth. "But I thought it might make me remember something if I said that."

Kali laughed and took a bite. She made a face.

"What, you don't like it?" asked Craig.

"No, I wouldn't say that – it's just not what I expected."

"What did you expect?"

She shrugged. "I thought that a gooey tendril would be inside."

Now Craig made a face at her. "That sounds horrible. If that happened we'd have to leave immediately."

Kali laughed loudly, eliciting a dirty look from the older couple sitting one table over. She looked down and Craig realized that her cheeks looked a bit pink.

Craig looked over. The old man was still staring at her, shooting daggers with his eyes. "Can I help you with something?" Craig asked with a smile.

The man huffed and returned his gaze to his wife's scowling face.

Kali kicked him under the table. "Craig – be nice!" she whispered.

"I am being nice! It seemed like they needed something."

Their meals came out just then – ridiculously huge portions on ridiculously huge plates. They took up the entirety of the table. Kali couldn't be more thrilled – she dove in and devoured half of her gnocchi before sitting back with a groan.

"I think I'm going to explode," she said.

"You're just getting started," Craig replied with a laugh. "Don't you want to try mine?"

"Just one bite, maybe," she said, reaching her fork across the table.

"And you need to save room for dessert."

"I can't! I'm so stuffed." She took a bite of Craig's pasta. "Oh wow – that's really good too."

"I'm not going to finish all of this," he replied. "Perhaps we can pack it up and you can have some tomorrow?"

"No, I'm not going to steal your food!" Kali said in a hushed voice. "I'm not usually this much of a pig."

"You could never be a pig," he said. "You're behaving exactly as I'd expect a woman to behave who's survived on 'sad single people food,' as you call it."

Kali rubbed her forehead. "Yes...yogurt, eggs, salads. It's all very healthy."

"That's all fine, but those foods don't feed the soul quite the same as gnocchi in a bread bowl, do they?"

"That they do not," she conceded.

Craig caught the waiter's eye and asked him for the dessert menu.

"Some boxes as well, sir?" he asked.

Craig looked at Kali.

"Yes, please," she said.

Once they had the menu, Kali admitted that she could do with a few bites of tiramisu.

"Your wish is my command," Craig said, standing up to find the waiter. He wanted to put in their order for dessert and also pay the tab. It was sweet of Kali to propose going dutch, but this was supposed to be his treat to her. It was only a drop in the bucket compared to what she'd done for him, but it was something, and he wasn't going to let her waste any more money on his behalf.

He successfully caught the waiter and handled the bill before returning to the table a few minutes later.

"Sorry," he said as he sat down, "had to go to the loo."

Kali snorted. "The loo!"

"Easy now," he said, raising a hand in surrender. "You'll make me self conscious."

"I'm sorry," Kali replied, rather seriously. "Do you remember when you woke up? You asked me if you were really English or if you might've woken up speaking – "

He covered his eyes with one hand. "Fifteenth century Italian. Or Vietnamese. Yes, I remember."

"Don't be embarrassed," Kali said. "It was funny!"

"I suppose it was. Unless I've been faking my accent the entire time."

Kali frowned. "That would be weird."

"Would it?" Craig responded in his best American accent. He wouldn't have risked that a few weeks ago, but by now she was familiar with his humor. Even if most of his jokes did make her roll her eyes.

"Doesn't matter, the tiramisu is coming," Kali said, eyes wide.

Craig laughed. She was now totally unfazed by him, which was somehow more charming than when she was slightly suspicious but still kind.

The waiter set the plate in front of Kali and she thanked him.

"Oh – there's only one fork," Kali said.

Craig hadn't noticed. He was staring at her again. "What? Oh, that's alright. I don't need any cake."

"You don't like tiramisu?"

He paused. "I'm not sure, really."

"Well – come over here and have some then."

She didn't have to ask him twice. He scooted his chair next to hers; the space was so tight that he could only fit if they were almost touching. She didn't seem bothered by this.

"Here," she said, cutting a bite of the layered cake. Placing one hand under the other, she carefully raised the fork to his mouth. It was a rather large piece.

"Despite this being the biggest bite of cake I can remember having," he said, mouth full, "this is quite good."

"I thought it might've been a bit too big, but it was too late. It was already airborne."

He caught her eye but forced himself to look away. Taking the fork from her hand, he cut a smaller piece for her. "Your turn?"

She opened her lips and took a dainty bite. Craig had the overwhelming urge to kiss her. A flake of chocolate lingered at the corner of her mouth. He took his napkin and raised it to her face.

She didn't stop him.

"You've got a little something," he said quietly.

"Oh, thank you," she replied.

He dropped the napkin, softly brushing the side of her cheek with his hand for just a moment. Her skin was so soft – to his surprise, she closed her eyes for a second.

Craig felt his heart skip a beat. He couldn't resist it any longer. He had to kiss her. He leaned in, slowly. He was almost to her lips when her phone rang.

Kali snapped away and cleared her throat.

"Sorry, don't mean to be rude, I need to get this."

"Of course," he replied, but she'd already stood up from the table and walked away.

Craig stayed at the table with his heart racing, staring at the slice of cake. Truth be told, despite taking a giant bite of it, he hadn't tasted anything at all. His focus was solely on Kali. He never intended to kiss her. He knew that she insisted they were just friends. How could he stick with that, though? Despite not remembering most of his life, he knew that Kali was the most amazing woman he'd ever met. He was sure of it. He could feel it in his chest whenever he saw her laugh. Or when he thought of her, late at night, when he couldn't go to sleep. She was all he thought about, really. How could he stay just friends when he was madly in love with her?

She came back to the table after a few minutes. She looked a little pale. Craig leapt up.

"Is everything okay?"

"Yes, everything's fine – it's good news, actually."

"Who called?" he asked.

"It was the police station," she said slowly. "They apologized for not calling sooner. But they have some footage of the night you were found. And they have your wallet. And they found – they have your name."

"My name?"

Kali nodded. "It's Craig. Craig Watson."

# Chapter 13

Somehow the tiramisu didn't appeal to her anymore. Kali sat back in her seat, a little further from Craig than before.

"Does knowing your name help you remember anything?" she asked.

Craig stared at the table, concentrating. "No."

"Do you want me to search your name on my phone?"

He looked up with a half smile. "Alright!"

Kali pulled out her phone and typed Craig Watson into Google. He leaned over slightly so he could look at the results.

"Let's see...are you this triathlete? Or this lawyer? Oh – or this boxer?"

"I don't think I have the nose of a boxer."

She laughed. After clicking on the links and seeing the men's pictures, she went back to the main search. "I don't think any of these are you."

"Maybe try adding Britain or something?"

Kali nodded and added it to the search. The first headline was from *The Sun*. "Billionaire Bad Boy to Wed Heiress."

She snorted. "Do you think *this* one is you?" She clicked the link. A picture of an elegant and rather expensively dressed young woman popped up.

"That's a lady," Craig quipped, "so I don't *think* that's me."

Kali scrolled down in the article and hit another picture. She froze. It was like her brain couldn't process what she was seeing.

"Kali," he said after a moment, "am I imagining things, or does that man look like me?"

Kali pulled the phone closer to zoom in on the picture. "Uh – it kinda does look like you." The shirtless man looked a lot like Craig – his hair, his smile. He had abs, apparently. Her heart rate picked up. She zoomed out and looked at the caption of the picture.

It read, "Craig Watson relaxing on the £30 million yacht he gifted his sweetheart."

Kali set her phone on the table. His sweetheart. Not only was he engaged to some sort of a beautiful model creature – he was rich. Insanely rich.

While she'd suspected that he came from money with the way he behaved, she'd *never* suspected something like this. The richest person she knew was a kid she went to high school with – Billy Marmalade – and he wasn't even that rich. His dad was a successful banker. They had a Mercedes and a private basketball court and a big pool attached to their giant house. To Kali, that was as rich as rich got. Yet Billy's dad was probably just a millionaire.

Ha, *just* a millionaire! Her mind kept racing. Luckily, Craig was distracted by reading the article and hadn't yet noticed her catatonic state. A logical voice in her head told her to pull it together, but another more powerful force made her feel cold and like she might throw up.

"I think we've found you," she said, trying to keep her tone bright.

Craig reached for the phone, staring at his picture again. "This doesn't make any sense. Are you sure this isn't some sort of prank?"

"I don't know for sure," she said. "But I don't think so."

Craig scrolled down to another picture of an older couple. "This says Phillip and Maggie Watson! I think these are my parents!"

Kali peered over. "I think you're right. See, you did remember her name."

"I remember them!" he said excitedly. "My mum – Maggie from Madison. My mum grew up in Madison!"

"Is that why you were here? To see family?"

He frowned. "I don't remember."

"Oh, that's okay. It's all coming back to you," Kali said, forcing a smile.

He grabbed her hand. "It is."

Kali quickly pulled away, pretending to straighten her hair. "We should contact your parents. I'm sure they're worried sick about you."

"Right," he said.

Kali cleared her throat. "And...your fiancée too." She tried to keep her voice steady, but it betrayed her at the end by fading out. She coughed to cover it up.

"Are you alright?" he asked.

She waved a hand. "Yes, I think I just got some of that powdered chocolate stuff in my throat. Should we get the check? I promised Ashley that I'd stop by tonight."

"Right, of course," he said. "Actually – I already got it. Sorry, I knew you'd never let me, so I took care of it earlier."

"Oh!" she said. Normally she would've scolded him for doing something like that, but she didn't have it in her now. It was the least surprising news of the evening that he'd snuck off and paid the tab. Seemed like a billionaire thing to do.

They gathered their leftovers and walked to the car in silence.

"I'll drop you off before I head over to Ashley's, okay?"

"Thank you," Craig replied.

Once in the car, the radio sprung to life with Adele's velvet voice.

*I know I have a fickle heart and a bitterness...and a wandering eye and a heaviness in my head. But don't you remember? Don't you remember?*

Kali switched the station. Rock music. She didn't know any rock songs, and she thought it'd be better that way.

"I'll probably be at Ashley's late," she said. "But feel free to grab my laptop from the living room. Maybe you can get in contact with someone?"

"It's the middle of the night in London," Craig said with a laugh. "So I doubt they'll pick up the phone."

"No," Kali replied, keeping her eyes on the road. "But you can send them an email, maybe? Let them know you're alive?"

"That's not a bad idea."

"I guess I don't have to worry about you stealing my stuff anymore," Kali said with a nervous laugh.

Craig turned to her. "Regrettably, my alleged wealth has no impact on my kleptomania."

Alleged. That was odd of him – there was nothing alleged about it. But it was easier to play along than have to face the enormity of the truth. "Ah, of course. That's where all of my forks have gone."

"No actually, those are all in the sink downstairs, sorry. I will return them. But I am a fan of your cats and can't make any promises about not stealing them."

Kali shot him a look. "My cats!"

"Chip in particular. The little rascal has taken a liking to me."

"Well I hate to burst your cat-stealing bubble," Kali said, putting the car into park. "But Chip would have to go through an extended quarantine to travel back to Britain with you, and I don't think he's up to it."

"Isn't he?"

Kali crossed her arms. "No. I already asked him."

"What did he say?"

"He said *Mrooowww!*"

Craig burst into laughter. "That does sound like him." He turned to open the door. "Well – thank you for the lovely evening."

Kali nodded. "The officer said we could go to the police station tomorrow to collect your things."

"Right. Thanks."

"Don't wait up," she said as he stepped out of the car.

"Have a good night!" he called out as he closed the door.


Kali pulled away, laughing to herself about her cat joke – Craig wasn't the only one who knew how to make lame jokes. Anyway, there was no way she would let Craig take Chip. If he were rich enough to buy a yacht, he could buy his own stinking cat.

Ashley only lived a few minutes away and by the time Kali got there, she felt totally better. It was good that Craig figured out where he came from. Great even! Sure, him being a billionaire was a bit of a shock, but that only meant that she didn't have to support him anymore. He could probably leave on his private jet tomorrow, in fact. She'd never have to risk being seen around town with him again and she could start standing up to Betsy. Life would return to normal, just like she wanted.

Ashley saw her pull up and came running outside. She peaked into the passenger seat.

"What, no Craig?" Ashley asked with a disappointed look.

"You're going to freeze to death!" Kali said, getting out of her car. "Where's your coat?"

"You sound like my mother!" Ashley lamented, pulling her into a hug. "Come here you big bad ICU nurse. I haven't seen you in *forever!*"

They walked into Ashley's house, arms linked. This was just what she needed to forget that she'd had a billionaire living in her basement for the past few weeks.

"So seriously, why didn't you bring Craig?" Ashley asked once they got inside.

Maybe it *wasn't* the right place for her to go to forget about Craig. "He's back at my place. The police called, they found his wallet."

"Get out! So he knows who he is now?"

"Sort of. He knows his name. And we found some stuff about him online."

"Oh my gosh – please tell me he's single."

Kali removed her coat, shooting Ashley a stern look. "Aren't you a happily married woman?"

"Yes, but you aren't. And Steven said he talks about you *all* the time."

Kali's heart made a little leap. All the time? She pushed the feeling away. "He's not single. He's engaged. And she looked very nice."

"I bet she did." Ashley slapped her in the shoulder. "Look at you in that dress! You look fabulous!"

"Ow!" Kali rubbed her shoulder. Ashley was stronger than she realized. "I just – I dug this out of my closet. Craig insisted on taking me to – "

"I know, Amalfi Corner. Steven told me. And I don't care how 'nice' this woman looked, there's no way she looked as nice as you do in *that dress!*"

"It's not like that, Ashley."

"Uh huh."

"It isn't! I didn't help Craig all this time so I could be some homewrecker."

"Aha!" Ashley pointed a finger in Kali's face. "So you admit it! You like him!"

Kali shook her head and answered in her level headed nurse voice. "No, not like that. He's a nice guy, and I'm glad I could help him out, but that's it."

"So you're not upset at all that he's going to walk out of your life forever and marry some woman who didn't even notice he was missing?"

"We don't know that!" Kali said. "He was very hard to find. He's here in Wisconsin, for some reason, and she's in London. Well, he thinks he's here because his mom was from Madison. He remembered that."

Ashley stared at her for a moment. "Interesting."

"What?" Kali said, exasperated.

"Nothing. Well, let's get some face masks on and then we can stalk him online."

Kali smiled. She wasn't against learning a little more about her soon to be ex-tenant. "If you insist. You're in for a surprise."

They spent the next two hours reading every article they could about Craig and his family. Kali felt bad – it seemed a bit intrusive. Ashley insisted that it was fine, especially when she saw that he was labeled a "billionaire bad boy."

"He's practically a public figure. We can't be the only two women in the world who don't know his business. And oh my gosh!" She gasped.

"What?"

"He took you on a date!"

Kali rolled her eyes. "He did not. It wasn't a date."

"It was *too* a date."

"Was not."

"Was too."

"I'm not having this argument with you!" Kali finally said.

"Fine," Ashley said with a knowing smile. "But we still need to look into his history."

Kali thought it was wrong, but she couldn't resist. Ashley found information about his parents, his school friends, and of course, his fiancée. Kali managed to act perfectly indifferent as Ashley gasped about this or that. By the end of the night, she'd played it off so well that she almost had herself convinced that she didn't care about Craig.

Almost. There was a moment – one she couldn't help, just when she got home. She pulled up to the townhouse and saw the glow of a light in her living room. Her first thought was that Craig might still be awake and she felt excited – she felt genuinely excited that she'd get to see him again. After hurriedly getting to the door and walking in, she found the room empty. He'd just left the light on for her.

Her heart fell. And in the solitude of her living room, she no longer had to pretend. She let the sadness flood in and she reminded herself that this was her life – Luke was gone, Craig would leave, and she would be alone for the rest of her days. That was how it had to be.

She quietly went upstairs and got ready for bed.

# Chapter 14

It was after eleven when Craig heard Kali come in. His first thought was to jump up and return her laptop, but after only a few seconds, he heard her go upstairs. He didn't want to follow her – that might scare her, plus he didn't know what to say.

All this time he'd lived off of her hospitality while secretly being rich. He worried that she might think he hid it on purpose. He certainly did not...though now that he knew the truth, he wished he could go back to not knowing.

The internet allowed him to learn a stunning amount of information about his life – his father was one of the richest men in Britain, and his family had been powerful landowners for hundreds of years. Towards the end of the nineteenth century, the Watsons also got involved in shipping, resulting in their wealth skyrocketing during the first and second world wars.

None of this was exciting to Craig – not really. As he read more, little bits and pieces of information came back to him. It all seemed – well, a bit embarrassing. His family profited off of some of the worst wars in history. Sure, they didn't encourage the wars or anything, but it seemed a bit boorish to make a fortune from it.

He remembered his grandfather James, though, did not find it boorish at all. He found a picture of his grandfather on Wikipedia and the memories came flooding back.

James was the exceedingly proud and cold force that ruled over the entire family. Craig's father Phillip wasn't going to inherit anything after disappointing his father by marrying an "American field mouse." When Phillip's older brother died unexpectedly, James was forced to leave him the family fortune. Otherwise, it would appear that the family unit was falling apart, and James cared very much about the appearance of the family.

Looking at pictures of his father and mother, Craig had a few fond memories trickle in, but it was like he was seeing them through broken glass. Things didn't connect, he couldn't hear their voices. They were just out of reach.

The one person that he couldn't remember, no matter how many pictures he looked at, was his fiancée Bernadette. He found her public Instagram, so he had *a lot* of pictures to look at. She was a beautiful woman, tall and lean like a model. Her hair was always perfect, at least in pictures anyway, and the pictures were always taken so she looked like she was having the most marvelous time. Craig must have stared at her pictures for two hours. Nothing came to him. Not her voice, not her smell. He couldn't think of her favorite meal or her favorite movie. It seemed like she liked to travel – she had pictures all around the world. There were even some of the two of them, on the yacht he supposedly gave her.

It was so strange for Craig to see pictures of himself on the yacht or skiing on a mountain top. Without his memory, it seemed like he was looking at an identical twin who led a much more glamorous life than he did. It didn't seem right. Just that week he pulled a glob of hair from a drain that was the size of his fist. As disgusting as it was, he was excited by it at the time. Not only did he solve a concerning drainage problem in the bathroom they were working on, but then he also got to chase Steven around the house with the glob, much to everyones' amusement.

There was one video on Bernadette's Instagram that was particularly cringe worthy. He was shirtless for some reason, running down the beach.

"No pain no gain!" he yelled as he ran by the camera, pointing at his abs. Bernadette, who was holding the camera, giggled.

Craig watched it three times, hoping that perhaps it was part of some inside joke. He couldn't possibly be that pretentious, could he?

He had to stop looking at things online. Everything he found showed him as a stuck up, self obsessed snob. Perhaps he wasn't getting the full story. That's what he had to tell himself, at least, to be able to fall asleep. He couldn't have been *that* bad of a person – his parents were lovely people. He did almost kiss Kali the night before, but that was only because he didn't know he was engaged. He'd be sure to keep things strictly professional with Kali going forward. Surely his memories of Bernadette would come back soon, and the love he felt for her would return from wherever it was hiding. He'd promised himself to this woman, after all, and he wasn't going to betray her because of a knock to the head.

The next morning, he felt awkward going upstairs to face Kali, but if she knew any links to his embarrassing identity, she showed no hint of it.

"Morning," she said cheerfully after he knocked on the door.

"Morning," he replied, watching her carefully. "Did you have fun with Ashley last night?"

"Yes, we had fun. Thanks for asking."

He cleared his throat. Was it him making it awkward or was she being awkward, too? "That's good."

"Were you able to contact any of your...family?"

"Yes," he said hurriedly, "I reached out to Bernadette, I sent her a message. Hopefully the police will have my cell phone, though, so I could contact some of them more easily. I can't remember anyone's phone number."

Kali frowned. "They didn't mention a cell phone. But we can head over now if you like? Do you want some breakfast?"

"I'm alright, thanks." He had no appetite. He was afraid that they'd find out even more terrible things about him at the police station.

He wasn't totally wrong. When they got to the station, the officer they met with first apologized profusely for not calling sooner.

"We actually found your wallet not long after you stopped in, but the officer on the case had to take an unexpected leave."

"Is he alright?" Craig asked, imagining the worst.

The officer smiled. "Maternity leave. Baby came a little early, but they're both doing fine."

"Oh," Craig said, feeling like an idiot. Why did he assume the officer would be a man? "That's good to hear."

"So we were working through her highest priority cases and... well, sorry."

Craig waved a hand. "It's no problem, none at all. I've had a very kind guardian these last few weeks." He smiled at Kali.

"The world needs more people like you, miss," the officer said to Kali.

She blushed. "Oh, it was nothing."

Hang on a minute. It seemed like this officer was *flirting* with Kali. That seemed unprofessional of him! Who did he think he was, flirting around on the job? Craig leaned in to read his name tag.

"Officer Wilkes, you said you had a video?" Craig said to break up whatever was going on between them.

Wilkes broke his gaze on Kali. "Yes, come this way."

The three of them walked back to a small desk. Officer Wilkes pulled a video up on the computer screen and hit play. Craig leaned forward. It seemed to be security footage of a street corner. After a few seconds, a figure walked onto the screen.

"That's me!" Craig said, pointing excitedly. "You have footage of the guys who attacked me?"

"You bet," Wilkes said with a smile.

Craig turned back to the screen just in time to see his huddled figure slip in a cartoonish fashion and fall flat on its back.

Kali burst out laughing. "Some attackers you had there Craig! It looks like it was the invisible killer: black ice."

Craig crossed his arms. "I was attacked by the brutal Wisconsin winter. It's claimed many victims, you know."

Wilkes leaned in to fast forward the video. He slowed as some figures approached Craig. "These are the individuals who found you. They called 911 – but they also stole your shoes and coat first."

"Don't forget my wallet and phone," Craig added.

Officer Wilkes nodded. He pulled a zip lock bag from his desk drawer. "We recovered your wallet next to a nearby dumpster. The phone was nowhere to be found."

"Thank you," Craig said as he pulled his wallet out of the bag. It was made of fine leather. All that was inside was his identification and a frequent buyer's card to a place called Dingo's Dogs.

"Oh this is exciting," he said, pulling out the card. "It looks like I'm only two hot dogs away from a *free* dog."

"It's really good they didn't steal that from you, Craig," Kali commented.

Officer Wilkes responded to her joke with a belly laugh.

"Well," Craig said curtly, "thank you for all of your help, officer. We won't take up any more of your time."

"You're welcome. Stay warm out there – and Craig?"

"Yes sir?"

"Try not to fall down again."

Kali burst into laughter.

"Right, thanks."

He had no right to be jealous of this officer flirting with Kali, so he decided it was best to excuse himself. If she were into that sort of muscular, brave, hero type of fellow then that seemed like a good match for her. Why shouldn't she have a good match? She certainly deserved it.

Hopefully Bernadette would see his message soon and arrange to bring him back home. Then he could leave Kali to her life and her flirting and never cause trouble for her again. It would be best for everyone if he left. The sooner the better, he decided.

# Chapter 15

Monday morning, Kali got two unpleasant surprises. The first was a phone call that roused her from sleep. She caught it just before it went to voicemail.

"Hello?"

"Good morning Kalista, sleeping in today?"

She looked at the clock. It was 6 AM, on the nose. "Morning Betsy." So typical. How dare she be lazy and sleep past six on her day off?

"Listen, I'm going to need you to come in tomorrow."

"Tomorrow?" Kali repeated, rubbing her eyes. She wasn't a morning person.

Betsy sighed. "Yes, tomorrow, as in the day after today."

"I can't. I'm scheduled off tomorrow, sorry."

"I'm telling you that I'm rescheduling you."

Kali gritted her teeth. She *knew* she requested that day off well in advance. It was Luke's birthday. There was no way she could miss it. She rushed downstairs to look on her laptop. "No, I can send you the confirmation email that I got that approved."

"No, I'm sure that you didn't," Betsy said. "I was being nice and going to cover the shift for you, but that doesn't work for me anymore."

"It's not covering my shift," Kali said, feeling anger bubbling in her chest. She found the email where the day off was confirmed. She couldn't keep the edge out of her voice. "I'm *scheduled* off. I just forwarded the email to you."

There was an urgent knock on the door – Craig clearly heard that she was awake and wanted to hang out at precisely that moment. He kept knocking, so she covered her phone before cracking the door open and gesticulating that he needed to keep quiet.

Instead, as soon as he caught her eye, he said, "Oh thank goodness you're awake, I need to – "

Her eyes almost bulged out of her head. Without thinking, she threw a hand up to cover his mouth. He gave her a puzzled look.

"Kalista..." Betsy asked slowly, "who was that?"

"Door to door salesman," Kali said quickly. "Did you get my email?"

"Do I need to remind you that you're on thin ice?"

Kali slowly pressed a finger to her lips to signal to Craig that he needed to keep quiet. He nodded.

"I'm not sure what you mean," Kali replied.

"I have a picture of you," Betsy said, lowering her voice, "*canoodling* with one of your former patients. Did you think I'd just forget?"

"Betsy." She made sure to keep her voice even. "I am scheduled off tomorrow, and I can't change my plans. Thank you for checking in."

"I heard him! I heard his voice! I know you have him there, did he *spend the night*? Or are you going to say it was some *other* British guy you picked up?"

Kali's heart started thundering. Was this all a bad nightmare? Why was Betsy so awful yet so perceptive at the same time? "I don't know what you're talking about." Her voice cracked, betraying her.

"Listen here *little miss thing*, you'll be here tomorrow morning or I *will* report you to the hospital ethics committee."

The line went dead. Kali felt the blood drain from her face. The ethics committee? She definitely didn't want to defend herself in front of them. But what if she had to? She wouldn't lie about Craig. She couldn't. When she told them the truth, they'd understand that she did the right thing. Right?

Craig approached her slowly. "I am *so* sorry. I didn't realize you were on the phone this early, and I really needed to talk to you because – "

The doorbell rang – a second unpleasant surprise. Craig froze. Kali gave him a puzzled look.

"Because?"

He cleared his throat. "I think that's for me."

She stared at him for a moment before she realized what he was saying. "Oh. Oh! Let me get it, they'll freeze out there!"

Kali hurried over and opened the front door to an elegantly dressed Bernadette McKinsey. She didn't know how to pretend that she hadn't spent two hours stalking her online with Ashley and that she didn't recognize her. Bernadette towered over Kali in a pair of stiletto heels; Kali looked up at her with her mouth slightly open. Bernadette slid her sunglasses down her nose.

"Hello there, I'm looking for Craig Watson?"

Kali practically jumped back. "Yes please, come on in! He's right here."

Bernadette strode past, her heels clicking on the hardwood floor. She had on some sort of long, draped coat and a fur around her shoulders. It looked like she walked out of a magazine.

"Craig, sweetheart!" She outstretched her arms when she saw him. "I've been so worried about you!"

"I'm sorry to have worried you," Craig said, stepping toward her. She delicately placed her arms around his neck and kissed the side of his face once.

"Are you alright? I came as soon as I got your message."

"Yes, I'm fine," he replied, blushing a little. "I'd like you to meet my – friend and hostess, Kali Mitchell."

Bernadette released Craig and turned around. "It's so nice to meet you. You can call me Bunny, all of my friends do. Thank you for taking *such* good care of my Craig."

Kali realized that she was standing there in pajamas that had ice cream cones printed all over the pants. Not exactly how she imagined meeting an heiress. "It was no problem."

"You are too sweet," Bernadette said, turning back to Craig. "Well then, are you ready to go? I have the jet waiting."

Craig's eyes darted between Bunny and Kali. He looked as surprised as Kali felt.

"Oh" he said, "I have work today. I can't just leave."

Bunny let out a laugh and tapped a dainty hand on Craig's chest. "Always the jokester. Come now, Craig, do you have any belongings you'd like to take with you?"

"No really, I can't leave without talking to Steven," Craig said.

Bunny popped her sunglasses into her purse. "I think my Birkin is going to freeze to death out here, I don't know how you stand it!"

"Birkin?" Craig asked, cocking his head to the side.

Bunny reached out and gently stroked his hair. "My goodness, you really must have had quite the blow to your head."

"Her purse," Kali interjected. She only knew this because Ashley found an article about how Bernadette – er, Bunny – paid $120,000 for the handbag that she now had casually hooked on her arm. It cost more than Kali's townhouse...the townhouse that she was still paying off.

"See, your friend Kali knows what I'm talking about!"

Kali cleared her throat. "I'm sure Steven will understand, Craig. I told him that you'd rediscovered your identity when I was visiting on Saturday, I mean, I think he knows."

"Oh," Craig replied.

Bunny slipped her sunglasses on the top of her head. "If you'd like to stay for a bit, that's fine with me. Just let me know and I'll arrange it with the pilot."

Craig looked down, then back at Bunny. "No – I suppose it doesn't make much sense for me to stay any longer, then. If you have everything ready."

"I do, but take your time. Here," she reached into her purse. "I've bought you a new phone and reloaded all of your contacts. I assume yours went missing?"

"It did. Thank you Bernadette."

"Oh Craig, please, call me Bunny. You do remember me, don't you?"

"Of course," he said. "It's just – in bits and pieces."

She touched his face lightly. "I'm sure it will all come back to you in no time!" Bunny flashed a beautiful smile.

Kali watched this exchange, her expression blank, as her stomach flipped around inside of her. Her feet were freezing standing so close to the front door and somehow it made her feel even more like a child, standing next to them barefoot. They looked like Barbie and Ken. But richer.

"Can I offer you some tea? Coffee? And Craig can get his things together," she finally said.

"Tea would be lovely, thank you."

"Kali," Craig said softly, "could I bother you to use your phone to give Steven a ring?"

"Sure." She handed him the phone before leading Bunny to the kitchen.

It was only a few feet away, and Kali never felt self conscious about how small her place was until that moment. It only took four strides of Bunny's long legs to get there. She set it out of her mind and instead focused on getting the tea ready. The kitchen was a mess, of course. It was on her radar to clean it – in fact, she planned to clean up right after breakfast and packing Craig's lunch. A pang of sadness hit her – she'd never get to hear Craig call it "the best, and heaviest, packed lunch this side of the Atlantic" again.

Bunny chatted pleasantly; Kali asked about her trip and how everyone took the news of Craig appearing again.

"To be honest, it's not unlike him to disappear for a few weeks at a time. He always turns up eventually," she said with a laugh.

"Oh."

"But this time, I knew something was different. I started to worry and sure enough, it wasn't long before I got his message."

Craig appeared in the doorway. "You know, I don't have much to take with me that's actually mine. I did want to say goodbye to Chip if I could."

"I'll see if I can find him," Kali said. She welcomed a chance to step away from the two of them. She felt like an intruder, even though she was in her own home. After a brief search, she found Chip cozily tucked in her bed. He must've climbed into the warm blanket after she got up abruptly that morning.

"Come here you little bed monster." She carried him downstairs, cradled in her arms like a baby. He loved being carried like that. He was an unusual kitten.

Craig scooped him up. "There he is, my furry little prince." Chip purred as Craig rubbed his cheek.

"My goodness, what a little angel!" Bunny said, standing up. "Don't tell me he's yours?"

"I found him under a car," Craig said. "Brought him home and promptly overran the place with fleas."

Bunny smiled. "Glad to hear you've been causing trouble wherever you go."

He planted a kiss on Chip's head. "Goodbye little man. I'll miss you."

"You can visit him any time you like," Kali said, stretching out her arms to take him back.

Craig smiled at her. "Kali – I don't even know what to say. You saved my life. Thank you a thousand times. You're welcome to visit anytime. I mean it."

She smiled. "Thanks Craig. Travel safe, okay?"

He nodded. "Will do."

"Take care Kali!" Bunny said before striding towards the front door.

Kali followed them, opening the door with one hand and cradling Chip with the other. They stepped outside and the cold air gushed through the doorway. A black Land Rover sat on the road, waiting. The driver hopped out and opened the back door for Bunny. She disappeared inside.

Craig turned around, a frown stretched on his face. He raised his hand to wave. Kali waved back, forcing herself to smile. He dropped his arm and stared for a moment before turning and getting into the car.

The driver closed the door. Within a moment, they set off. Kali watched as the car disappeared in the distance. Once she could no longer see it, she closed the door and slid the lock into place.

Chip wriggled out of her arms and ran back upstairs. He wanted to get back in bed before Kali did.

"Little stinker," she muttered as she watched him bound up the stairs.

She went back to the kitchen, feeling far too awake to fall back asleep. The problem was that there wasn't much for her to do. Kali sat at the kitchen table, staring at her tea. Maybe she would visit someday.

Sure. Why not? It'd be fun to have friends in London. She'd never been outside of the country before, and perhaps Bunny could take her shopping and show her how to be fashionable. It'd be nice. It'd all be really nice.

That's what she told herself, at least, so that she wouldn't keep replaying that look on Craig's face before he got in the car. What was that? Sadness? Regret? He probably missed Chip. He'd get over it. Soon he'd be back to his fabulous life. And she'd be back to her own life, like nothing ever changed at all.

Nope, nothing different at all.

# Chapter 16

When Craig stepped onboard the jet, he felt like a little kid.

"This is so cool! Can I talk to the pilot?"

Bunny gave him a puzzled look. "Whatever for?"

He shrugged. "Dunno. Maybe I can be the copilot."

"And kill us all? No." She pointed him towards a seat. "Settle in and don't cause any trouble. Your mother wants you to stop in for dinner when we land."

Craig sat down. "What time does she expect us?"

"Oh, I can't make it. You'll have to press on without me." She lowered a sleeping mask over her eyes. "I need to catch up on my rest just now."

Before the plane took off, Bunny was sound asleep. Craig was disappointed; he'd hoped to ask her at least a hundred questions, but he decided she must be behind on sleep after flying out to pick him up. He stared out of the window, watching the buildings fade into the distance. He finally found out who he was. He knew he should be happy – but why did it feel like his heart was sinking into the plane's cargo?

Trying to push the feeling away, he leaned back in his seat. An attendant stopped and asked if he'd like anything. "Some fresh strawberries?" She suggested.

It felt strange to send this poor woman for strawberries, so he politely declined. Instead he pulled out his new cell phone and scrolled through the contact list. It was full of names that he didn't recognize. After debating for a minute, he added Kali's number – he didn't want to forget it, plus he may need to talk to her for one reason or another in the future. At this point, she was still one of the few people he actually knew in his life.

He took a picture of himself and sent it to the contact labeled "Mum."

"Coming home!" he wrote.

She responded instantly. "Can't wait to see you XOXO KISS KISS!!"

Craig cracked a smile. He didn't have a memory and even he knew the X's in XOXO stood for kiss. Or perhaps it was the O's?

The plane provided an internet connection, which Bunny made sure was already connected prior to giving him the phone. He grew tired of looking at it after about half an hour. Bunny was still asleep; it'd be unkind to wake her for his own entertainment.

Instead, he went to the back of the plane to chat with the two attendants. At first they seemed startled, as though he were going to reprimand them for something.

"Really I'm quite bored," he confessed. "I don't mean to intrude, is this a staff only area?"

The attendant laughed. "No sir, you can go wherever you please."

He waved a hand. "Please don't call me sir – Craig is fine. Do tell me, how does this little drink cart work? Where are the brakes?" He knelt down to examine the fancy, and very heavy, looking cart. Ever since working with Steven, he developed a special interest in understanding how things worked. He'd come a long way since not knowing how to unbolt a toilet.

Craig spent the next few hours chatting with the attendants and eventually made his way up to see the pilot. He was surprised to find the pilot so welcoming, allowing him to take a seat while patiently explaining the various controls and screens. After not too long, Bunny came to get him.

"I was worried when I woke up and you were gone!" She said. "I was afraid you'd run off on me again."

"Never," he said with a smile.

He finally had the chance to talk to her. First he admitted that he still had many gaps in his memory, so he asked her to tell him some of the basics – where she grew up, what she did for a living...what *he* did for a living.

"You're a businessman, of course. As am I."

"Where do I work?" he asked.

She laughed. "You don't have to work. We don't have to go to absurd 9 to 5 jobs like everyone else."

That didn't make much sense but he didn't know what to say. He settled on, "Oh."

She waved a hand. "And you have many advisors that will practically run the company for you once your father passes away."

Craig retracted, surprised. "Is he ill?"

"No, of course not. I just mean – you know, when you are to inherit."

"Oh, right." He paused for a moment, unable to decide if he should share the thought that just popped into his mind. Oh, why not? "Kali secured me a job while I was in Wisconsin. A friend of hers was a contractor. On my first day, he told me to take a toilet of the floor. I had no idea how to do it, didn't even know how to take off the tank lid."

"Oh that sounds horrible," Bunny replied. "I hope you've showered since working on all of these toilets."

"I haven't, is that a problem?" he said with a smile.

She sighed. "There's a shower in the back of the plane. Do freshen up."

"I'm only joking!" he said. But she was already engrossed on her laptop.

"Sorry dear," she said, "I have a lot of work to catch up on."

"Not a problem."

They landed not long after and on his way out, Craig thanked everyone and told them that he hoped they'd see one another soon. Bunny reminded him that this was one of his planes, so he could see them literally whenever he wanted by ordering the plane.

"That's not very nice," Craig said without thinking. "I should give them some sort of a schedule, don't you agree?"

Bunny scoffed. "What else do they have to do with their time?"

Craig couldn't tell if she was serious – but it seemed like she was.

They walked off of the plane and towards the two waiting black cars.

"This is where I leave you, my love," she said, planting a kiss on his cheek. "We will catch up tomorrow?"

He smiled. "Of course." He opened the door to her car and watched as she pulled away.

Craig enjoyed his ride home. Some of the sites seemed familiar to him while others seemed brand new. Memories of his parents trickled back in pieces – and he was disappointed when he realized that he didn't have a big family like Kali. He was an only child, actually.

There were some cousins that he was particularly fond of, and plenty of aunts and uncles as well. But no little brothers or sisters. That much he remembered.

What he still could not remember, no matter how much he tried, was anything about Bunny. He didn't know how they met or how he proposed. There were no memories of her family, or of any of those international trips that she'd documented so well on her Instagram. Somehow, she remained a black spot on his mind.

As the car pulled up to his parents' house, Craig saw his mother and father standing outside, waving frantically. The sight made him laugh out loud. They didn't look like two of the richest people in the country – they looked like any other pair of overly excited parents welcoming their child home.

They pulled him into a hug as soon as he got out of the car.

"Hello mum, dad!"

"Welcome home son!" His mum squeezed him so hard that he found himself out of breath. "Well let's get inside, you'll freeze to death out here!"

He laughed. "This is nothing compared to Madison this time of year."

"You'll have to tell us all about it!"

They went inside and sat down at the dining table. Craig's mother fussed around, fetching things from the kitchen until the table was full. He'd forgotten how much she loved to cook. She'd made his favorite – spaghetti bolognese. She'd also baked fresh bread (which he knew was from scratch) and put together a lovely salad with vegetables from her greenhouse.

Once all of the questions about the flight were out of the way, his mother asked him to tell them everything that happened. "From the beginning," she urged.

Mouth full of bread, he started. "Unfortunately, I still don't know what happened the night I er – well, at first I thought I was attacked. Turns out, I slipped on some ice and knocked myself out."

His mother gasped. "How awful!"

"I'm okay," he said gently. "I found this out later when the police showed me a surveillance video. Slipped and fell. Some passersby relieved me of my coat, wallet and shoes before calling for an ambulance."

His father let out a laugh. "You were defeated by a patch of ice, then?"

"Oh yes, completely. And at that point, I was taken to hospital – to intensive care. I woke up rather quickly, as I understand it, but had no memory of who I was or how I got there."

His mother made a tsk noise. He continued. "By the next day, they transferred me to a room with a man who I'm sure, by now, is dead, judging by his terrible cough. I decided I should excuse myself, so I found my way out."

"Craig William Watson!" his mother gasped. "You did not!"

"I did," Craig said hurriedly. "They did say that I was ready to be discharged that day. Funny thing was, I ended up giving them a fake name and didn't have a way to face the bill."

"Don't worry Maggie," Craig's father said evenly. "We'll make a donation to cover his stay."

She sighed, wagging a finger. "You've always been a rascal."

Craig smiled. That was one way to put it. "Long story short, I underestimated the Wisconsin winter and found myself in need of shelter that night. I made it to the men's shelter, but it wasn't to my liking – "

His father laughed again. "I would quite like to see you in a men's shelter."

"The smells alone drove me out," Craig replied with a shudder. "I ended up at a food bank to get a meal. As luck would have it, the nurse who cared for me in the ICU was there. And she – well, she had a basement flat she'd finished and planned to rent. But she allowed me, quite graciously I might add, to stay there while I sorted out my situation."

"There's that midwestern charm that I so love," his father commented. "I'm sure she wasn't much to look at, but it doesn't matter since it sounds like she had a heart of gold."

"She was beautiful, one of the most beautiful women I've ever seen in my life," Craig said without thinking. The surprised look on his parents' faces told him that his comment may have been an over-share.

"Not that it mattered, of course. She was exceptionally kind." He filled them in on the details of her foster cats, her siblings, his cat and subsequent fleas, and finally her fiancé who tragically died of leukemia. When he finished, they both stared at him for a moment.

"Well, she sounds like a lovely person," his mum said.

Craig smiled. "She was. I mean – is."

"It seems we are quite in her debt for returning you to us safely."

"Yes, but she wouldn't want anything, of course."

"Of course," his mother agreed.

He decided to change the subject. "Why was I in Madison to begin with?"

His father answered. "For the gala."

"What gala?"

"I'd asked you to attend in my place. I can't tell you how I've regretted it," his mother said with a sigh. "It was a gala to raise money for some Madison-based charities."

"Ah," Craig said. "Because you're Maggie from Madison."

"That's right," she said excitedly. "You remember!"

"It was the first thing I remembered, actually. But it wasn't very useful without a last name."

She laughed. "I suppose not. Well anyway, I attend every year, but thought it'd be nice if you saw where I grew up. Bunny went with you. She said the night you disappeared that you told her, 'Don't wait up.' "

Craig frowned. "That does sound like me. Have I always been such a terrible git?"

His mother grabbed his hand. "You're not a git! A rascal, sure. But never a git."

"Sure, mum. Dad?"

"A bit of a git, yes," he responded. They erupted into laughter. "But not much worse than I was at your age."

"Fair enough," Craig said.

They sat for another few hours and he told them about his escapades in toilet and tile work. They found every story hilarious, but after a while, he was too tired to give each story justice.

"I'll need to hear some of those again," his mum warned him as she headed up to bed. "And I won't be able to sleep until you tell me the name of the lovely girl who took you in. I have to send her a thank you note."

Craig obliged. He wrote down her name and address on a sheet of paper. "Alright mum. But nothing embarrassing, promise?"

She held up her hand. "What was it that you used to say when you were little? Pinky swear?"

He gave her a kiss on the cheek. "Yes. Goodnight mum."

"Sleep tight."

Somehow, he didn't trust that his mother wouldn't do something embarrassing with Kali's information. She did pinky swear, though, and there had to be some honor left in that.

# Chapter 17

After a fair bit of worrying, Kali decided to call Betsy's bluff. That Tuesday, she did not go in for work. Instead, she visited Luke's parents, went to his grave, and lit a candle for him. She knew she'd requested the day off and she could prove that to anyone who questioned it. It was unacceptable to keep living her life under the threat of "exposure." Most importantly, she did what she needed to do to honor Luke's memory.

Betsy's response came in early on Wednesday. Kali was scheduled for the 7 AM shift and her phone rang at six – it was someone named Sue.

"It's come to our attention," Sue said, "that there are allegations of your improper conduct with a patient."

Kali heard herself gulp. "There are?"

"Effective immediately, you are suspended. We'll be in contact with a date for a hearing in front of the ethics committee."

She didn't know what to say. Clearly now wasn't the time to argue. She settled on, "Thank you," and "have a nice day."


Not knowing what else to do, she called her mother, who was outraged by the allegations and threatened to go down to the hospital and confront Betsy.

"Please don't," Kali said. It was nice to have someone on her side, even if they seemed set on the unrealistic plan of inciting some sort of a riot. They talked for a good bit, her mother reassuring her that the investigation would find that she acted honorably, and therefore, she should enjoy this free vacation. Kali laughed. It didn't feel like a vacation. It felt like they were taking away the most important part of her.

Kali thought of texting Ashley, but knew she was at work already – plus, would they pull her texting logs or something for the hearing? It was better to leave no trace. Instead, she sent Ashley a text message that she'd gotten some bad news. This caused Ashley to become outrageously curious; she stopped by Kali's place on the way home from work.

"Spill the beans!" she said. "I've been imagining terrible things all day!"

"Oh, it's nothing. Well, not nothing – I'm being investigated for 'improper conduct.' Right now I'm suspended."

Ashley sat down dramatically. "I thought you were dying or something!"

Kali frowned. "Not literally. But if I can't be a nurse..."

"Stop. They can't take away your license. I don't think." Ashley shrugged. "Worst case, you may get fired."

Kali groaned. "That's pretty bad."

"It is," Ashley said, "but it's not the end of the world. Listen, if they fire you, I'll go to a new hospital with you! I'll quit in solidarity!"

"You don't have to do that," Kali said. "I know you love your floor."

Ashley shrugged. "Not as much as I love you. And don't worry, I'm sure they'll scold you and nothing will come of it. Slap on the wrist."

"When they find out he was living with me, I'm sure that I'll get more than – "

"How are they going to find that out?" Ashley said.

Kali eyed her for a moment. "Well, if they ask."

"No! Don't tell them anything! All they have is what, a picture?"

"Yeah, but – "

"But nothing! Innocent until proven guilty."

Kali sighed. "I don't think it works that way."

"Well then, stop thinking so much," Ashley said, crossing her arms. "You'll get yourself in trouble."

There was a knock at the door. Kali shot Ashley a puzzled look. Who could that be? A little streak of terror shot through her that it may be Bunny again. Did she forget her ridiculous purse somewhere? That reminded her – she needed to tell Ashley about seeing it.

Kali opened the door – it was a delivery guy.

"A letter for you, ma'am. Please sign here."

"Uh – okay. Thank you."

"Have a good night."

Kali closed the door and examined the large envelope in her hand.

"Who's it from?" Ashley sat up with interest.

"It's posted from the UK," she said slowly. Had Craig sent her something? A little flutter of hope took off in her chest.

"Well don't just look at it! Open it!" Ashley urged.

Kali carefully opened the envelope, slipping out a single sheet of paper. Ashley jumped up to read over her shoulder.

*Dear Kali Mitchell,*

*Thank you a thousand times over for taking care of my son Craig these past few weeks. I grew up in Madison, and I know how brutal the winters there can be. If you hadn't opened up your home to Craig...well, to be honest, I'm too afraid to think of what may have happened to him. Thank you does not seem like enough.*

*My husband Phillip and I request the honor of your presence in our home in London. I would like to properly thank you in person. I understand that you lead quite a busy life, however, I can send the jet whenever is convenient for you. Please feel free to bring any guests you so choose. Craig has told us all about your wonderful mother, father, sisters and brother, and your best friends Ashley and Steven. Everyone is welcome to join.*

*I have included my phone number at the bottom of this letter. Please feel free to reach out to me at any time.*

*Truly in your debt,*
*Maggie Watson*

Kali stared at the letter for a moment, quickly re-reading it. What on earth? There was no way she was going to go to London. She needed to be in the country so she could defend herself from being fired.

"She knows my name!" Ashley said excitedly. "That's so cool!"

Kali laughed. "Don't get any ideas."

"Hold on, just hold on a minute," Ashley said quickly. "Think about it! You can't go to work. I have to work the weekend and then I'm free next week. What could be more perfect?"

"What could be more perfect? Me getting my job back!"

"Oh relax, you haven't lost your job yet." Ashley outstretched her hand. "Can I see the letter?"

"Fine," Kali said, rubbing her forehead. She didn't want to be rude and refuse to go, but at the same time, she was absolutely not going! It was absurd and out of the question. How would it look to the committee if her patient sent a *jet* for her? It was one of the most ridiculous things she'd ever heard, and she'd have none of it. Who did Maggie Watson think she was?

Ashley returned the letter to her. "Well, I've got good news and bad news."

"What?"

"The bad news is that I didn't know how to text internationally. The good news is that I figured it out and told Maggie that we're ready to be picked up next week."

Kali's jaw dropped. "You didn't."

She giggled. "I did!"

"Ashley! How could you do that?"

"Listen Kal, I need to go home and do some laundry. What's the weather like in London?"

"We are *not* going to London! And why did you invite yourself?"

"She practically sent the letter personally to me! She knows I'm your best friend."

"She also thinks Steven is my best friend."

"No," Ashley said, pulling on her coat, "clearly Steven is Craig's best friend. Duh. But he can't come, he has to work."

"Ashley."

"I suggest you buy some new clothes before we fly out, you're going to stick out like a country bumpkin in London!"

Kali gritted her teeth. "I'm not going to London."

"Good thing Luke made you get a passport, now you can finally use it!" Ashley said brightly. "And I haven't used mine since my honeymoon."

"I don't think – "

Ashley cut her off, patting her on the shoulder. "I know we'll look back on this one day and laugh."

"No, we won't!" Kali said, arms crossed.

"Love you, sleep tight!" Ashley scooted out of the door before Kali could say anything else.

Kali sighed and went back to look at the letter. She couldn't very well message Maggie Watson now and say that it was a false alarm. It looked like she was taking her suspension to London after all.

# Chapter 18

Though he hoped to have at least a day to recover a bit from jet lag, Craig found himself running wedding related errands with Bunny for the rest of the week. "You've gotten out of helping me for far too long," she reasoned.

He didn't think that was quite fair, but he said nothing. Instead he tried to gather as much information about this wedding as he could. It seemed like he was paying for most, if not all, of the festivities. This became clear after he handed his credit card over more times than he could count that week. There were over 500 invited guests – close friends, family and business connections from both of their families. When Craig commented that it seemed a bit excessive, Bunny scolded him. "It was your idea to invite everyone you'd ever like to do business with!"

He had no retort. That probably was true, and apparently the invitations already went out, so it was too late to nix a few hundred people from the list.

The most absurd task that Bunny brought him along for was a photo shoot. For it, she changed into two different dresses. Craig didn't want to ask how much those cost him.

"Isn't it bad luck for me to see you in your wedding dress before the wedding?" he asked.

"This isn't my wedding dress silly," she replied. "It's my reception dress. There's no bad luck about it."

"It's quite poofy for dancing," he observed. "And looks heavy." It was covered in sparkling white jewels. Craig wondered if they were diamonds. That seemed like a waste.

"Beauty is pain." She carefully positioned herself following the photographer's instructions. Craig stood to the side, watching. He was dressed in a tuxedo. Someone came and put gel in his hair. Another woman tried to dab makeup on his face but he shooed her away. Is this how he used to spend his time?

Eventually the photographer pulled Craig in front of the camera and gave him instructions on how to stand and hold his arms. It was rather boring, and Bunny was dissatisfied with many of her lone shots, so she did them again. They repeated the process with her second dress.

"This is my leaving dress."

"For leaving...the country?" he asked.

"No, for leaving the reception. When they wave us off."

"Ah, I see. It's much lighter, for travel, is that it? We don't want to risk bottoming out the car as we exit."

She ignored him and stood still for makeup reapplication.

Craig took a seat on a nearby couch. He couldn't possibly have agreed to all of this. What were these pictures for anyway? Wouldn't they get enough pictures on the wedding day itself? He sighed and took out his phone. There was a message from his mum.

"Be sure to be home for lunch tomorrow, I've got quite the surprise!"

"As long as it's not wedding related, sure."

"No problem there!" she said. She added five hearts to the end of the message, which made Craig smile.

The photo shoot went on for another two hours, and he was so exhausted by the end that he forgot to ask where these pictures were going. He wished Bunny a good night and headed home to his parent's house. Bunny thought it was odd that he didn't want to return to his flat in London, which was closer to where she lived. He didn't know how to explain it to her, so he said that his mum asked him to stay over. In truth, there was something comforting about being home with them. They were still the main two people that he had memories of. Everything else was still trickling in. His flat in London seemed cold and empty by comparison.

He got home late and then stayed up until four in the morning watching things on Netflix. He was having a hard time adjusting to the time change, and also, he didn't like going to sleep. He kept having nightmares about freezing to death in Madison. In his dreams, he walked miles in the snow without seeing a single person. Sometimes he'd catch sight of Bunny, but she'd be just out of reach and she couldn't hear him calling her name over the whistling wind.

He awoke that morning just before noon and quickly rushed into the shower. He didn't want to be late for lunch so he made it quick. He was already dressed when he heard a knock at the door.

"Craig honey, it's me."

"Come on in, mum."

She opened the door and quickly shut it behind her. "Oh good, you're awake."

He ran the towel over his hair. "Yeah. Still getting over the jet lag."

"Well listen dear, your father and I have some guests over."

"Oh, for this surprise lunch?"

"Yes." She walked over and opened his curtains to let the sun shine through. There wasn't much sun, but it brightened the room a bit. "I invited Kali and Ashley to thank them for helping you."

Craig stopped dead in his tracks. "What? Here?"

"Where else?" She took the towel from his hands and walked to hang it back in the bathroom. "Ashley was quite enthusiastic about a visit."

He couldn't process what she was saying. "When are they getting here?"

"They arrived this morning. I sent the jet for an overnight flight. Your friend Ashley loved it so much that she called her husband just now to tell him."

"Oh, that's nice," Craig replied. He was only half there. He felt like his thoughts were running off without him.

"We'll see you down for lunch, then?"

"Yes, of course. I'll be right down."

His mother left and he went to look at himself in the mirror. He rubbed his forehead. He didn't want to look like a rich jerk in front of Kali – even if that's what he was. Everything he'd learned about himself to this point only made him feel embarrassed. It was enough to have to bear it in his own mind, let alone in front of humble, kind Kali.

She didn't need to know, for example, that his tuxedo for the wedding cost almost fifteen thousand pounds. Or that they were inviting 500 people. Or that Bunny arranged for the guests to receive gold trinkets as wedding favors. What else would Kali learn about his grossly lavish life? It was better when she was in Wisconsin, and the only Craig she knew was Craig Daniels, the hospital escapee. The real

Craig – whoever he was – didn't seem like someone that Kali would like at all.

He stared at his reflection in the mirror and wiped away the drop of sweat that formed on his forehead. The last time he looked at himself like this – really looked – was when he first got to Kali's place. He remembered feeling strange that he didn't recognize himself. It was now replaced with a much worse feeling – a sort of panic in recognizing what a fraud he was.

After a few minutes, he gathered his thoughts and decided that he'd go downstairs, have lunch, say hello, and then go back to his flat in London. It would be nice to see Kali, of course, but he'd make some excuse as to why he couldn't stay long. It'd be better this way.

The plan held out for a full minute – the time that it took him to get downstairs. Then he saw Kali. She was huddled in the kitchen, holding the hand of Mary, one of the house cooks. Her dark hair was off to the side in a loose braid. There was a flower tucked behind her ear, and her blouse had some sort of a sparkle, or perhaps the light from the window was hitting it just so. A little puff of air filled his chest.

"Just one second more, I can wrap it so that you don't have to worry about it getting wet." She turned around and saw him staring. "Oh Craig! Hi!"

"I didn't know you had a license to practice nursing here," he said, a smile breaking across his face.

She narrowed her eyes "No one has to know."

He approached her and she seemed to extend her arms to hug him. He leaned in and accepted the hug – her hair smelled delicately of lavender.

"Thanks for coming, Kali," he said. "My mother's been dying to meet you."

She turned back to Mary and continued her work. "It was very nice of her to – "

"Craig!" Ashley yelled, throwing her arms around his neck. "You're alive!"

"Hey Ashley, it's good to see you again. Thanks for flying out."

"No problem, that plane of yours is *amazing!* I slept like a baby."

"Glad to hear it."

Craig's mother stepped into the room. "All fixed up, Mary?"

"Yes ma'am!" she replied cheerfully. "We should keep this nurse on staff!"

"She might be available," Ashley interjected.

Craig turned to Kali, the question dancing in his eyes.

Kali shook her head. "It's nothing."

"Thank you, Kali, for your help," Craig's mother said with a warm smile. "Are we all ready for some lunch then? Phillip will join us later for dinner."

"Well I'm starving," Ashley said.

Kali tried to shoot Ashley a look, but she was already headed towards the dining room.

Craig was in a daze. Somehow it felt like it'd been years since he last saw Kali, but at the same time, it was as though he never left her in the first place. It made no sense. To add to his confusion, she smelled distractingly nice, and he wasn't used to seeing her wearing such pretty clothing. She was a beautiful woman no matter what she wore, of course, but he was used to seeing her bundled up in sweaters or in her nursing scrubs. Even though everyone complained about the weather in London being wet and dreary, it was nothing compared to Madison at this time of year. To them, it probably felt positively balmy.

As they sat down at the table, Ashley began what seemed like an exhaustive interrogation. She asked Craig's mother about where her family was from in Madison, their house's history, and the Watson family-owned lands. Craig spoke up now and again to address some of the questions, which allowed him to steal glances at Kali. He noticed that Ashley hadn't eaten much of her food.

"We're not known for our cuisine," he said, dropping his voice, "but you don't have to make it so obvious to Mary."

Ashley laughed. "I've just been talking too much to eat. This is delicious." She quickly tried to shove a large bite of curry into her mouth. It gave Craig a chance to change the course of the conversation.

"So mother, what sort of activities were you planning for our friends today?"

She shrugged, carefully taking a sip of water. "I wasn't sure. I'm happy to show them around town, but I thought it might be better if a younger person did it. I'm sure they don't want to be dragged through museums all day."

"Oh, I love museums," Kali said.

"Well that's too bad," Craig replied, "because I wanted to give you a proper tour of Soho and save you from dying of boredom."

Ashley nodded. "Yes, let's do that."

"But there's so much history – " Kali protested.

"Listen, I'll point at a few old buildings and make up some stories, and really what is the difference?"

They all laughed. Craig kept his eyes on Kali. He suspected that she may not be so easy to convince.

She sighed. "Alright, I guess it's your turn to show off your city. If you can remember anything about it."

He clapped his hands together. "Perfect. Of course I can. Berlin, right? Let's get started?"

# Chapter 19

"Yes, let's!" Ashley replied, standing up from her seat at the table. "Mrs. Watson, this was a *lovely* lunch. Thank you again!"

"Yes, thank you so much Mrs. Watson," Kali added. Though she was still mad at Ashley for making her go to London, Kali was grateful that Ashley at least smoothed over any awkwardness with her enthusiasm and habit of talking endlessly about anything.

"Please," she waved a hand, "call me Maggie. And it was my pleasure. I'll see you three later for dinner then?"

"Yes yes, mum, we can torture them tonight with a plate of bubble and squeak."

Ashley instantly made a face.

"It could never be as good as the oatmeal you were inspired to make me after going to McDonald's," Kali said.

Maggie turned to him. "You started cooking in Madison?"

Craig laughed. "Hardly. I managed to make oatmeal and a few sandwiches. Never got the hang of boiling eggs, though, and now I'm out of practice."

"I'm sure Mary could whip you back into shape!" Kali said.

His cheeks seemed to flush a little – odd, Kali didn't think what she said was that offensive.

"I'm sure she could," he replied.


He led them to the garage and told the driver, who apparently just stood around the garage all day, that he'd be driving himself.

"Very good, sir. Allow me to fetch the keys."

Ashley gasped. "Is that a Bentley Mulsanne?"

"It is. You have an eye for cars, Ashley?"

"Well – yeah! My dad's a mechanic. So I'm pretty much an expert, do you want me to change the oil for you? I'll need you to ship it to Wisconsin, of course."

Craig let out a laugh. "Gregory, can we please have the keys for the Mulsanne?"

"Right away, sir."

"Shotgun!" Ashley yelled, running to the car and touching the door handle.

Kali bit her lip not to laugh. She'd always admired that about Ashley – she behaved the same way in front of her best friend as she would in front of the Queen of England. Her patients adored her for it, too.

Kali never felt that free – she thought she had to hold back some part of herself, unless she was with people who knew her very well. In her mind, if she slipped up or did something embarrassing, only her closest friends could forgive her. And only then could she forgive herself.

Craig accepted the keys and unlocked the car. He opened the passenger door for Ashley. "Madame?"

"Wait, isn't this the driver's – " She looked at the car for a moment and burst out laughing. "Oh yeah, you guys drive on the other side of the car for some reason. Well, this is super weird."

"You called shotgun, Ash," Kali said. "So you're going to have to deal with it."

She sighed heavily. "You're right. Somehow I'll have to manage." She slipped into the leather seat with a broad smile.

He softly closed the door before opening the back door for Kali. "I hope the back will be comfortable enough for you."

Kali peered inside. "Not as comfortable as my Civic, but it'll do."

He laughed, gently taking her hand to help her in. It felt like a current ran through her body, warming her. She let go of his hand and straightened her jacket.

Craig pointed at a panel of buttons. "Feel free to make full use of the recliner."

Kali looked around, a bit startled. "Are you serious?"

He winked and walked around to the driver's seat.

The car came to life with a purr and Craig smoothly pulled onto the road. Kali felt like she was back on that luxurious jet.

"Tell me ladies, would you prefer a driving tour or a walking tour?"

"Walking," Kali said at the same time that Ashley said, "Driving."

He laughed. "How about this, we'll drive around a bit and then I'll leave the car for the second half of the tour."

Ashley crossed her arms. "Fine. But if the car gets stolen when we leave it unattended to walk around, that's on you."

Suddenly, Kali heard a noise behind her. She turned around to see the back window disappear.

"Uh – what just happened?"

"Sorry!" Ashley said. "I think I pressed a button I shouldn't have."

Craig laughed. "No, that was me. I didn't want Kali getting too hot back there – since she's fully adapted to a much cooler climate."

"I didn't know back windows could do that," she said, eyeing it suspiciously. The window quickly reappeared.

"I think we should get the touristy things out of the way via car – Big Ben, Buckingham Palace..."

Kali knew she was outnumbered, but she needed to try to plead her case. "Oh, but wouldn't it be fun to sign up for a tour to get the expertise of a guide?"

Craig and Ashley simultaneously replied. "Nah."

Kali rolled her eyes. She was stuck with them for sight seeing. It was a bit of a dreary day, but who cared when there was so much to see?

"Trust me," Craig said, "you'll see a lot more this way. This is your personal bus tour. With your own personal Brit."

"Can I see the Churchill War Rooms from the car?" Kali asked.

"Sure," Ashley replied, "just look at the ground and they're under there somewhere, right?"

Kali shook her head. She wouldn't get anywhere with these two. She decided to sit back and enjoy the sites. The city was truly breath-taking.

Craig skillfully drove them around and to his credit, he pointed out a number of landmarks. It started raining heavily not long after they started out, and Kali admitted that she was glad that she was in the car.

After about two hours of driving, the rain seemed to be slowing down and they decided to drop the car off at Craig's flat. He pulled into an underground garage filled with other fancy looking cars.

"Tell me these aren't all yours," Ashley said with a groan as she opened the door.

Craig scratched the back of his head and squinted at her. "These aren't all mine?"

"You're kidding me!" She threw her hands up. "That wasn't convincing at all."

"If it makes you feel any better," he said, leaning against the Bentley, "I don't remember where the keys are, so I can't drive any of them."

Ashley crossed her arms. "That does make me feel better."

"We can exit right over here…"

Kali knew nothing about cars. As far as she knew, these were no different than what she saw covered in slush in Madison. She eyed the elevator. "Does that go right up to your apartment?"

"Er – yes, it does."

She tried to suppress a smile. "I think I need to take a look. I brought some fleas, actually, and I'd like to return them to you."

He rubbed his hands together. "Did you tell customs that you'd brought live animals over?"

"Yes, they took the bed bugs from me, unfortunately," Kali said, striding towards the elevator. "But I still have some of Chip's little friends." This was one attraction she couldn't miss – the apartment of mysterious Craig Watson, bad boy billionaire.

"We'd best not keep them waiting, then," he said, calling the elevator.

They stepped inside and quietly went up a few levels. The doors opened to reveal a breathtaking view of the city with floor to ceiling windows. The hardwood was a rich chocolate color which contrasted stunningly with the crisp white walls.

Kali took a step inside. She wanted to crack a joke but couldn't think of anything to say. The apartment was immaculate. All of the details, everything from the exposed brick in the kitchen to the shining gray stone counter tops, made it look more like a movie set than an actual apartment.

She turned around. Craig looked so perfect here. This was where he belonged – in this elegant world. Not in her basement. Not touching her hand ever so gently to help her in and out of cars. She tried to push the thought out of her mind.

"Let's make a deal, Craig," Ashley said, hands on her hips. "If I find the car keys, I get to keep one of the cars."

He laughed. "Deal."

She squealed with delight and rushed off to pull open doors and drawers.

"She's never going to find them," he muttered. "I'd be glad if she did, though."

"This is really pretty," Kali said, looking out of the window.

"Would you like to see the balcony?" he asked. "It's right over here."

She looked around. "Sure."

He pulled open the door and she stepped outside. The rain stopped and they had a wonderful view of all the excitement and activity below.

She took a deep breath. "This is incredible. Definitely better than the view from my basement."

He shrugged. "I liked your basement. Quite a lot, actually."

"Sure." She cleared her throat. "Is Bunny going to move in here after the wedding?"

He crossed his arms and looked off at a building in the distance. "I don't suppose so. I heard her say that I agreed to sell this to get something – what did she call it? More feminine, I think it was."

Kali laughed. "Is she not a fan of the six car garage you have down there?"

"I'm afraid not. Trouble is, I rather like this place."

"Then keep it," Kali replied. "You can afford this *and* a more 'feminine' place, right?"

He flinched. "Yeah, I suppose. I don't know, really. I think this wedding may bankrupt us all."

She laughed a little too hard. Way to make it weird. "That's how all weddings are these days," she said hurriedly. "At least that's what I hear."

"What kind of wedding were you and Luke planning?"

"Oh," she said softly, "I don't know."

"I'm sorry, I didn't mean to – "

"No, it's okay. It's not – it's just that he was sick, so we never really had a chance to plan anything."

"Oh, of course."

She leaned against the railing. "I think we would've kept it small. A few people at the church, just our families and a few friends. It wouldn't have been big – Luke was an only child. And then – well, I always dreamed we could all take a trip somewhere. All of us, families too. We never went on vacation when I was a kid. It wouldn't have to be anything fancy – I'd like to stay in a big house together with everyone. We could stay up at night by the fireplace and tell stories, drink hot cocoa." Kali felt herself getting carried away by the power of her own nostalgia. It wasn't even real, but it made her heart feel full.

"That sounds lovely," Craig said. He took a step towards her and looked out onto the city beside her. "I'm so sorry you lost him, Kali. You deserve to be happy, you know."

Kali felt tears pooling in her eyes. There was a lump in her throat. She needed to nip her emotions in the bud before it got any worse – she took a breath before saying, "Thanks. Are you ready to show us Soho, Mr. Watson?"

"Of course, Miss Mitchell. It would be my honor." He opened the door for her to step back inside.

They found Ashley checking under couch cushions. "I have no idea what you did with those keys, man. There must be some sort of hidden compartment in one of these walls." She knocked on a nearby post.

Craig laughed. "Yeah, it's one thing to misplace your keys. It's another to hide them so well that a blow to the head erases all memory of their existence."

"It's those Wisconsin winters," Kali said brightly. She success-fully managed to avoid crying. She didn't know what about that balcony made her feel so strange and emotional, but she decided to avoid thinking about it. "Now – how far is Soho Square?"

# Chapter 20

An hour before dinner, Craig announced that it was time to head back. He hated to cut Kali's sightseeing short, but they got rained on when they walked over to the Palace Theater and he wanted to be sure they had enough time to get ready for dinner.

He was quite amused by the walking tour – it was almost entirely narrated by Kali. Apparently, she read some nursing book about how the eradication of cholera started in Soho. Craig had a vague memory of learning that in school, but not to the detail that Kali knew it. She did not, however, know as much as he did about the music scene in Soho – likely because it started long after cholera was eradicated and was of little interest to her. He talked about Trident Studios and Ronnie Scott's, she talked about the Broad Street water pump. Ashley complained that she was hungry and needed a rest.

They got back to his parents' house and he pulled up to the front door to return the car to Ted, the chauffeur on duty. He ran up to open the front door for them, then followed them inside. There was no sign of his mother, which was a relief, because he did bring everyone back later than promised and he didn't want to be scolded. He was about to run up to his room when he heard his name called out.

"Craig! There you are!"

He froze. Bunny. He forgot he'd invited her to join them on the tour and for dinner. She never answered his text, so he assumed she wasn't coming. "Hello, you!" He turned around and saw her standing in the foyer.

"I have the most terrible news."

"What happened?" he said, coming back down the stairs.

"They just called to tell me that they may not have *any* of the tall crystal vases available for the flower arrangements!"

He crossed his arms. "Terrible luck. Uh – where were those going again?"

"In the bathrooms! Honestly, it's like you're not even paying attention."

He let out a small scoff. "Well, that is a shame but it seems that the show must go on."

"Luckily," she continued, "the planner found another company that rents them but it's nearly double the price for them to bring them to and from the wedding."

Craig shrugged his shoulders. "Perhaps the bathrooms don't need flowers."

Bunny narrowed her eyes at him, but before she could respond, Craig's mother walked in.

"Hello darling!"

He gave her a kiss on the cheek. "Evening mum. Sorry we're late, I was going to just hop in the shower and then I'll be down."

"You're freezing! Did you forget to bring an umbrella?"

"Didn't even think of it."

She made a shooing motion with her hands. "Well run upstairs and warm up, dinner will be ready soon enough. I've got a nice surprise for our guests as well."

"As long as it's not one of dad's pranks – "

"Oh, that ship has sailed," she replied. "Go!"

He looked at Bunny. "We can figure out the vases later, alright?"

She nodded placidly, but Craig could tell that only his mother's presence saved him from a long argument about the necessity of bathroom flowers.

He went up to his bedroom and took a short, but wonderfully hot, shower. He wasn't sure what to wear with this surprise that his mum had in store. She loved surprising people, which led to some awkward outfits, like not having a swimsuit when she surprised him with a pool party when he was nine. He decided to put on some comfortable jeans and a short sleeved shirt.

When he got downstairs, the look on Bunny's face told him he chose poorly.

"Did you leave all of your sport coats in America?" she asked with a wry smile.

He looked down at himself then back at her. "Do you know what I should wear for this surprise?"

She sighed. "No, but I can't imagine that an outfit appropriate for riding rodeo bulls is what you'll need."

"But I don't even have a cowboy hat," he protested.

"You might as well," she snapped.

His dad walked into the room, so he decided to ignore her comment and instead assess how much his parents knew about the great cholera outbreak of 1854. Predictably, his mum knew the most, his dad knew some things, and Bunny didn't participate in the conversation.

Ashley and Kali came into the dining room not long after this discussion finished. He was caught off guard by the lovely white dress that Kali wore. She had a shimmering sort of glow about her again, only highlighted by the blush in her cheeks when introduced to his father.

"Phillip Watson, a pleasure to meet you," he said, voice slightly muffled.

Craig walked around the table to see what his father was up to. His words sounded a bit slurred and he was talking louder than usual.

"Ashley Miller, nice to meet you!"

"Hi Mr. Watson, I'm Kali." She extended her hand. His dad accepted it with a broad smile and a nod.

Facing them, Craig realized why his dad sounded funny – he'd put in his fake teeth again. Dad thought it was hilarious to put in these ghastly, crooked teeth whenever foreigners visited. He once sat through an entire dinner with a distant Canadian cousin, unable to eat anything that required chewing, just to run the joke that Brits had bad teeth.

"Dad, would you do me a favor?" Craig asked.

"Of course, son."

"Would you whistle the royal anthem for our guests? I told them what a spectacular whistler you are and they've been dying to hear it."

He nodded dutifully before trying to narrow his lips, but the fake teeth were too big. Despite starting to laugh, he tried to push some air through the teeth. He succeeded only in launching a bit of spit at Kali.

He erupted in laughter, causing the teeth to pop out. Kali and Ashley started laughing, too, once they realized what he'd been up to.

Craig's mum shook her head, but a smile danced at her lips. "Thank you honey, that was beautiful. Shall we all have a seat, then?"

"Yes, now that we've all had a bit of theater," Bunny said quietly, so only Craig could hear.

He gritted his teeth. Some vivid memories of Bunny not enjoying his dad's humor flashed through his mind – but what was he supposed to do? Tell his dad he couldn't joke in his own home? He hoped dinner would go quickly so the mood didn't grow tense.

As soon as they sat down, his mother started asking Kali all kinds of questions about the sites they saw, adding in bits of her own history knowledge. They seemed to be a match made in heaven – both lovers of history and all the boring bits of cities.

Craig sat between Ashley and Bunny and had a first row seat to all of Ashley's well meaning but poorly executed conversation starters.

"Is that a *real* Birkin?" Ashley asked Bunny.

Bunny, in all of her high bred charm, responded with a little laugh. "What else would it be?"

"I dunno," Ashley said, making a face. "I heard somewhere that those bags can cost a hundred *thousand* dollars! Or more! I've never heard of anything so crazy in my life."

"Yes, well, it can be hard to understand quality the first time you see it," Bunny said with a sweet smile.

Craig felt his body tense. Bunny could deliver a gashing insult in the prettiest of tones. Often her victims didn't know what hit them until later.

"True that, sister," Ashley said with a nod. The conversation continued with Bunny discussing her father's favorite thoroughbred horse. Craig felt himself relax. Good – no fight would come of this. Ashley continued to smile politely, asking questions about the horse or his special saddle when appropriate. But there was a moment –

just one moment – where Ashley locked eyes with Craig, and he thought he sensed a sort of sarcastic look on her face. It quickly disappeared.

They survived the rest of the meal without further incident. Craig was disappointed that he couldn't hear more of what Kali and his mother were talking about, but he was just too far away. Finally, as dessert came out, his mother decided it was time to tell them all about her big surprise.

She set down her glass and clasped her hands together. "I'm not sure if you remember this Craig, but I have a good friend at the Victoria and Albert Museum."

It didn't ring a bell, so he just smiled at her.

"Well," she continued, "I've arranged for us to have a few hours – alone – in the museum tonight after they close to the public!"

Kali was the first to respond. "Oh my gosh, that's *so* awesome!"

A smile broke across Craig's face. "That's one way to put it." He looked to Ashley, who sat there with a smile on her noticeably closed lips.

"What a treat," Bunny commented before taking the tiniest bite of her dessert.

"Another elegant surprise by my beautiful wife." Craig's dad leaned in and gave her a kiss on the cheek.

They piled into two cars to get to the museum; at first, it seemed that Craig and Bunny would travel alone, but he urged Bunny to pick a larger car so they could ride with Ashley and Kali.

"They're lovely people," he said quietly. "I would love for you to get to know them a bit better."

"Oh, of course," she responded. "Let's ask Ted to fetch the Rolls."

They got to the museum and found it well lit but eerily empty. Kali took off with Craig's mother – they were like two girls in a candy shop.

"You have to see the textiles collection, we have pieces from Predynastic Egypt!"

Ashley wandered off with Craig's dad to look at the sculpture hall. Craig trailed behind his mother and Kali, enjoying the occasional gasps of excitement that he heard Kali make. Bunny dragged behind him for a bit before sitting down to commit to texting on her phone more fully.

"You're lucky I'm so involved in planning this wedding, you know," she told him as she sat down on a bench.

"I certainly am," he said with a smile, leaving her behind to continue observing Kali discovering the museum. She was so happy that it made him feel quite bad that he refused to take her to a museum earlier in the day. This was much better, though – there weren't hundreds of other tourists around to get in the way of her discovery. After about two hours, the non-historians of the group grew restless.

"You've done wonderfully with this one, Maggie," Craig's dad said. "But perhaps it'd be best if I took the others home for some tea."

"I think I'll stay," Craig said. "I haven't made my way to the ceramics yet, and I loved them as a kid."

"No no," Bunny chimed in. "I've got a surprise of my own waiting."

"Is that right?" He looked at her with a raised eyebrow.

"It is right. Perhaps we can make our way back now?"

Kali stepped into the circle. "As much as I'd love to stay, I think we should all go and let the poor employees have a chance to get home to their families."

"Huh," Craig said. "That's a great point in favor of getting out of the museum. Ashley, what do you think?"

Ashley, caught mid-forehead rub, replied, "Yes, definitely. Just what I was thinking."

"I suppose you're right," his mother relented. "But we will just have to come back another time!"

"Absolutely," Kali said. "This museum would take weeks to know properly. Maybe years."

"I've lived nearby all my life and never managed more than an hour at a time in here," Craig said. "So for me, I'm coming up short-handed on a lifetime of visits."

Everyone laughed and made their way back to the cars. The ride back was quiet – it was dark, and everyone was tired from the day's activities.

Tea was set up for their arrival, along with some savory pastries and sweet treats. Craig watched Kali's eyes light up. It was the opposite of sad, single people food – it was rich, British tea food. He decided not to tell her that now, though.

Halfway through tea, Bunny disappeared. After a few minutes, she triumphantly reappeared at his side.

"There, look at this!" She held out a newspaper to Craig.

"What's this about?" he asked, accepting it. He opened the paper and to his horror, a full page photograph of himself and Bunny stared back at him.

"Let us see, then," his dad said, stretching out his hand. Craig didn't know what to do, so he handed it to him. That's what the photo shoot was about – some sort of publicity thing?

"Lovely hair you have son," his dad commented. "Did they photoshop it that way?"

His parents burst into laughter. Ashley took a peek and let out a giggle as well. Craig felt himself laughing. The only two who weren't laughing were Bunny and Kali.

"Perhaps his hair isn't in its best condition," Bunny said with a frown, "but I think it's rather impressive, don't you?"

Ashley set her teacup down. "Oh yes, splendid!"

Craig shot her a look and mouthed "splendid?" Her smile was unfazed. Luckily Bunny was too distracted telling everyone how difficult it was for her to secure this spot to notice.

Craig looked over at Kali. She looked pale. "Are you alright?" he asked quietly.

She seemed to startle. "Me? Yes, I'm fine. A bit wiped out from all the sightseeing. I think I'll head up to bed actually."

She thanked his parents for their hospitality and made a graceful exit. Bunny was still explaining to Ashley the exclusivity of the photographer, stressing in a very downplayed, British way of how big of a deal it was. Ashley feigned obtuseness about it. Craig didn't join in, partially because he didn't know anything about the photographer. Most of all, though, it was because he was distracted, thinking of brutal winters, lost kittens, and tiramisu.

# Chapter 21

After practically running up the stairs, Kali safely got back to her room without being stopped by anyone. She was afraid that Craig might come after her, but apparently she'd been convincing enough. Then she felt silly for thinking that he'd come after her. She was a silly, silly girl, harboring inappropriate feelings for a man who was very, very taken.

The picture of Craig and Bunny in the newspaper really took her by surprise. It's not like she forgot that they were engaged and getting married soon – but it was one thing to know it, and an entirely different thing to see it blasted on paper like that. It looked like a wedding photo, actually, with Bunny in a white dress and Craig dressed in a tuxedo. She was so impossibly elegant and beautiful, and he was so stunningly handsome. They looked perfect together, and it made her feel like she was going to faint.

And Kali was not an easy fainter. She'd seen a lot of things over the years as a nurse, lots of blood and bones sticking through skin. Nothing rattled her anymore, yet somehow this picture of Craig almost made her lose consciousness.

After he left Wisconsin, it was true that she missed him. It was nice having someone around, she reasoned. It didn't mean anything. When Ashley accepted the invitation, Kali was annoyed. She certainly wasn't plotting some way to see Craig again. At the same time, it was exciting – she'd never left the country before, and she loved Britain's rich history. It was an incredible stroke of luck that

Maggie was such an avid historian, too. She and her husband were both such kind people, not at all how Kali thought they'd be. She secretly thought they'd be snooty and treat her like some sort of peasant, but they were friendly – more than friendly, they welcomed her like some sort of hero.

And how did she repay them? By pining after their happily engaged son!

After her near fainting episode, Kali was forced to admit it to herself. Yes, she had feelings for Craig. She liked him. He was very likable. It didn't *mean* anything, though. It was like a schoolgirl crush, she told herself. Who wouldn't get a bit infatuated with a handsome, fun and goofy guy like Craig? All it proved was that she was still human, not that they had some special connection or something.

Yet here she was, halfway across the world, trying to find little ways to tease him, coming up with any bit of history she knew to talk to him about, lamely trying to impress him with her deep knowledge of cholera. Cholera! What a romantic topic! She was a great flirt, obviously, spending all day talking to him about a disease that caused unstoppable, deadly diarrhea.

Bunny would never talk to Craig about diarrhea. Bunny probably never even uttered the word diarrhea in her life. She was a real lady – classy, elegant, and beautiful. Her hair never looked messed up, she knew how to apply foundation so it looked seamless and she could walk around all day in high heels without ending up barefoot. Kali could never live up to that.

Nor should she try. She'd been in love once, and she knew that was all she would get in this lifetime. Perhaps if she came back in another life as a bumblebee, or a dolphin, or an emperor penguin – maybe then she'd have a new soulmate. Actually, she didn't know if any of those animals mated for life, but whatever. She'd met her soulmate, and she lost him. It was the greatest joy and the worst pain of her life. She wasn't going to go through that again – she couldn't go through it, obviously, since there was a one-soulmate-per-life limit.

Being a homewrecker and causing a rift between Craig and Bunny was not the way to repay the Watson's kindness. That would be exactly the kind of unladylike behavior they'd expect from a paper mill owner's daughter.

Kali decided that she could not control how she felt, but she could control how she behaved. This little crush on Craig would go away. All she needed to do was put some distance between them. She'd go back to Wisconsin, he'd get married, and their little bit of time spent together would fade into the past.

It was a nice time, sure – but honestly, she only knew him for a few weeks and how could she think she was in *love* with someone after that? He didn't even know who he was the whole time! It was absurd. It was infatuation, a crush. She was sure of it, and she was sure of her decision to leave as soon as possible.

Kali talked to Maggie the next morning before breakfast – she thanked her profusely for the amazing visit, but said that she and Ashley really needed to get back to Wisconsin as soon as possible. Maggie tried to convince her to stay, but Kali wouldn't budge. She was sure in her decision. Ashley too tried to argue to stay, but she told her that this was what needed to be done and she'd explain later.

She felt fine with her decision as they said goodbye. She felt fine with it when Craig pulled her in for one last hug and she took in the delicate smell of his cologne.

He insisted on driving them to the runway and she felt fine getting out of the car, stepping on the staircase to the plane, waving goodbye and taking her seat. As the plane sped through the sky, each mile added between her and Craig only made her feel more at ease.

Everything felt perfectly fine and Kali had no doubt in her decision. She knew she did the right thing, even if it made her a bit sad. She took comfort in it. Ashley didn't ask any questions, which surprised her, but Kali decided not to push it.

They landed in Wisconsin and Steven came to pick them up. Ashley told him all of the details about their trip, almost in a single long stream of words. Kali laughed and added comments in here and there. When Steven got to Kali's place, Ashley insisted on walking her to the door. Kali thought that was odd, but nice of her.

"Gotta make sure no one broke into your place and is waiting there for you," she reasoned.

Kali opened her front door and once she proved it was entirely deserted, Ashley was satisfied. Or so Kali thought.

"One more thing, Kal."

"What's up?"

Ashley sighed. "I didn't want to say anything. So I'm just going to say it and run back to the car."

Kali knew what she was going to say, and she was ready with a rebuttal. "Listen, Ash, I get that you – "

"No! Just one thing and I'm running. I know your heart shattered when Luke died. I *know*. But he wouldn't want you to use his death as an excuse to run from love for the rest of your life."

Kali opened her mouth to protest but was too shocked to think of anything. This wasn't what she expected from Ashley.

Ashley continued. "You can't be so afraid of getting hurt that you miss out on life. Especially when life gives you a really, *really* amazing chance at being happy." She smiled and squeezed Kali's hands. "Okay, I love you, and I'll talk to you tomorrow, and I'm not going to let you argue with me, goodnight!"

Ashley turned and ran back to the car. She almost slipped and fell on the ice, but with some wild swinging of her arms, she recovered. Kali watched from the doorway, mouth still slightly open.

All this talk of her being *afraid*...that wasn't true at all! Kali wasn't afraid! She just – knew better than to expect more from life. She already had more than her fair share of love.

She closed the door and tried to busy herself with unpacking. No matter how busy she kept herself, she couldn't ignore the heavy feeling in her heart. What was she supposed to do with that?

# Chapter 22

Craig watched the plane take off and fade into the distance. He was going to miss Kali. He knew it was wrong to feel that way when he was engaged to another woman, but it was still true. It seemed like rain clouds blew in overhead as soon as she left. He drove home in silence.

His mum greeted him when he got back.

"What'd you think of your surprise visitors?"

He smiled. "It was lovely to see them, mum. You're still the queen of surprises."

She clasped her hands together. "Oh, good! They're both such lovely people. And Kali is just as beautiful as you said she was."

Craig felt himself flush. "Yes, well, I've got to get going. Bunny requested that I taste more cakes with her. Apparently the ones we picked out are no longer acceptable forms of cake."

She looked at him for a moment before replying. "Alright sweetheart."

He drove to pick Bunny up at her flat and they headed off. It was a struggle to find parking near the caterer, and they ended up having to walk several blocks, much to Bunny's annoyance.

"I don't see why you couldn't have dropped me off first, *then* gone to get a spot."

Craig shrugged. He was enjoying the walk. "It was too late – by the time I found it, if I went to drop you off and come back for it, it'd be gone."

"Next time," she said with a flat tone, "let it be noted that I will *not* walk for half an hour to get a parking spot."

"Noted." He looked across the street and saw a young couple smiling and holding hands. Craig wondered if he and Bunny ever held hands. Now was not the time to try.

Suddenly he heard a shriek. He quickly spun his head to look at Bunny, thinking there was something wrong. Instead he saw a big, bounding dog being dragged away from her.

"My apologies," the owner said.

Her jaw was tight. She didn't look at him again, but instead muttered to Craig, "That filthy animal almost got its paws all over my coat."

Craig froze. He remembered this. This wasn't the first time he saw a dog jump like that...

First, his memory of being knocked over by Kali's family dog ran through his mind. His brain was trying to show him all of the jumping dog memories, as if they were important.

In a flash, he had another one – walking with Bunny on a dark Madison street. Yet another jumping dog – this one succeeded on leaping onto her coat. It replayed in his mind like a scene from a movie:

"Ugh!" she'd muttered in disgust. "He's gone and covered my coat in mud!"

"It'll be alright," Craig responded. "We'll wash it off when we get there."

"I don't *want* to arrive filthy," she said. "Go back to the hotel and bring a towel. *Now!*"

Craig didn't argue. He turned around at once to fetch a towel for her.

That was when it happened. That's when he slipped and fell on the ice. He remembered the exact moment leading up to falling – he remembered his annoyance with Bunny, he remembered the bitter cold in the air.

And Bunny? He closed his eyes, trying to remember what happened after his fall. Was she there? Did she look for him? He didn't get far from her, perhaps a block, before he fell. The hotel wasn't far. Surely she saw the ambulance rush past, surely she wondered...

Bunny's voice snapped him back into the present.

"Craig, what are you doing?" she asked, annoyed. She was several yards ahead of him, apparently she hadn't noticed that he stopped walking.

His voice was low. "I never said 'Don't wait up,' did I?"

She looked around, confused. "I only took a few steps, Craig. We're going to be late."

He shook his head. "In Wisconsin. The night I went missing – you said that I told you not to wait up for me. But that's not true."

She took a few hurried steps towards him. "Of course it is, you must've forgotten."

He pulled away from her. "I *remember*. How could you have left me there? After you sent me to get a *towel?*"

Bunny sighed. "Come now, Craig, what are you going on about?"

"I could have been dead!" he said, voice rising. "And you just left me there!"

"Yes, but you *aren't* dead, are you? You're completely fine! The ambulance picked you right up and whisked you away to your dear little nurse. Is that what you wanted from me? To dress like a custodian and fuss over you until you were back to health?"

"So you saw the ambulance?" He waited for her to respond. She didn't, so he kept talking. "No, I didn't want you to be my nurse, but I didn't expect you to leave the country."

She crossed her arms. "Are we going to make it to this cake tasting or not?"

"Not," he said, turning and walking away from her. "Call yourself a car when you're done," he called out behind him. He knew it was rude to leave her there, but it was still not as bad as when she left him.

He went back to the car and drove to his flat. Once there, he didn't know what to do with himself. He tried turning on the TV, but there was nothing interesting to watch. He thought about texting one of his friends – he started to remember them as well, but he wasn't sure what he talked to them about before. From what he remembered, they didn't seem like people you called up just to chat with. Ski or take a two week yacht trip? Sure. But talk about a fight you had with your significant other? Not really.

Craig turned off the TV and sat with his face in his hands. He didn't have a genuine friend in the entire country. He did nothing during the day because he had no job or work to keep his mind occupied. And his fiancée was a woman who apparently saw nothing wrong with leaving him with a head injury in a strange city. This was the life he built for himself. No wonder he didn't want to remember it.

Frustrated, he decided to go for a drive through the countryside. He'd always enjoyed doing that with his dad when he was a kid. He swapped cars to something sportier – his Ferrari. Luckily he'd finally remembered where the keys were. Ashley was right, they were in a secret compartment. It was a good thing she hadn't found it, though, because the keypad would've been rather demoralizing for her.

He took off in his car and put on some music. He drove for two hours until he got a call from his mum asking if he'd like to come by for dinner. He told her that he would, but it might be a while before he could get back.

"Still can't decide on cakes?" she asked with a laugh.

"Something like that," he replied.

The drive helped him feel marginally better. He had one missed call from Bunny – just one. She was too proud to ever beg or plead. She knew that when he was ready, he'd come and talk to her. It quite annoyed him, actually, because he felt that she had a lot to apologize for.

While driving, he tried to remember why he was with her. No matter how hard he tried, he couldn't remember many nice things about her. He knew that her family was also extremely wealthy and that combining their properties would make them financially unstoppable. But that was no reason to get married, was it?

Being rich made him a bit of a target – he learned that the hard way in his younger years with women who were clearly after his wealth. Bunny at least had money of her own, so she wasn't after him for that. It wasn't really clear what she was after. A nice wedding, that was a start. She was beautiful, of course, and elegant. There was nothing wrong with her, not on paper at least, though her personality was colder than he liked.

Finally he settled on the fact that she was likely the best that he could do. It wasn't like he was some great guy. Why should he deserve to be with someone thoughtful and kind when he himself was selfish and lazy?

He spent all of his days thinking about himself and himself only. It didn't help that he was rich – he certainly attracted the wrong sort of person – but there was nothing else attractive about him. He was a spoiled, rich brat. Bunny was exactly the sort of woman he deserved. Maybe better than he deserved really. This was the life that he made for himself.

He arrived back home in a sour mood. Dinner with his parents was nice, but he had a hard time engaging in conversation. He was still stuck in his own head. His mother made his favorite dessert, shortcake with ice cream, and grew concerned when he didn't devour it like usual.

"Is everything alright, Craig?"

He nodded. "Yes, everything's fine, why?"

"Did you and Bunny have some sort of fight over the cakes?"

She was too good at figuring things out. He decided it was better that his parents never know that his bride-to-be left him for dead, especially if he couldn't find anyone better to marry, because he was the same caliber of person. "No, not really."

"Ah, alright."

"I wonder how Kali's getting on," his dad said, mouth full of ice cream.

"What do you mean?" Craig asked.

"Oh," he shrugged, "Ashley told us she had some sort of a hearing coming up at work."

"You're joking," Craig said, setting down his spoon. "With the ethics committee?"

"Yes, that's it! In two days, I think. Seems that she was quite worried about it."

Craig sighed. "I can't believe that. It's because of me. She risked her career taking me in, and now she'll pay the price. And for what?"

"That's one way to think of it," his father said with a frown.

His mother jumped in. "What are you talking about, of course she had to take you in! You would've died!"

Craig shook his head. "It's not how they see it. The ethics board, I guess."

"Well then you have to set them straight," his mother said decidedly.

He scoffed. "How? By shaking my trust fund at them? Fat lot of good it did for her to stick her neck out for me. She's going to lose her job for someone who's never had a job in their life. How do you like that?"

"That's a rather fatalistic way of looking at it," his dad observed. He was not the sort of man who liked to talk about serious things. If he did, he preferred it to be in a joking way. Craig knew that he was being a bit too dramatic at the moment to suit his dad's normally light hearted take on things.

"You know, Craig," his mother said, staring at him, "if you don't like the way things are, it's never too late to change them. Nothing is set in stone."

He shrugged. What hope was there for him? He was the worst kind of man – the worst of the worst. He didn't do anything unless it was to further himself. The only woman he could convince to marry him was, he was pretty sure, heartless. He didn't have a true friend in the world. Well, he did once, but then he messed it all up with regaining the memory that he was a crap person.

She reached out and touched his arm. "I mean it, son. You've certainly come back...a bit different after hitting your head. Not better, not worse, but – different. It's like you grew up overnight."

He gave her a weak smile. "Have I moved on from being an overgrown toddler to being a moody teenager now?"

She smiled. "No, you're moving on from having the mindset of a boy to thinking like a man. And I'm glad for it! You don't have to be ashamed of who you were. You should be ashamed to sit around and do nothing with your new knowledge. And best of all, you can keep your old thinking from affecting you for the rest of your life. If you act fast enough." She winked.

Craig gave her a puzzled look, but she simply stood up and kissed him on the forehead. "Why don't you stay over here tonight? I'll make you that oatmeal you liked so much for breakfast."

"Alright mum, goodnight."

His dad sat there, finishing off his dessert. After a moment he said, "And son, do something about that Bunny of yours. She came by the house today behaving absolutely feral."

"Really?" Craig said with interest.

"Indeed. She was screaming something and pounding on the door. Your mother refused to let her in. Said that she was afraid it was the first known case of a rabid rabbit."

They both laughed. His father stood and gave him a pat on the shoulder. "The jet is at your service, should you need it."

How did his dad know that even with the amusing image of Bunny going ballistic, all he could think about was flying to Madison?

Better not to ask. "Uh – thanks dad," he responded.

Craig turned back to his shortcake. It seemed he was at a cross-roads. His mother was right – he could either sit here, wallowing in self-pity, or he could do something. Anything. He could just *try* to be a different person – a better person.

He had a lot of work to do and there was no time for delicious desserts. Well, maybe he had just a second to spare – he took two big bites to finish it off before he went upstairs. There were calls to make.

# Chapter 23

The morning of her hearing, Kali got up extra early; she didn't mean to, but the entire night she kept waking up every hour, terrified she'd oversleep. By five in the morning, she gave up – there was no need to risk missing the hearing for an extra few minutes of sleep.

After taking a shower, she ate breakfast and stood in the kitchen, sipping on coffee. There was nothing left to do in the house. She'd been off of work for far too long and in order to keep from going crazy, she fully cleaned her townhouse from top to bottom. She fixed the lock, finally, that connected the kitchen to the basement; she cleaned all of the animals' cages; and she dusted every picture on her wall. That was sorely overdue, actually, and she was a bit embarrassed by how much dust collected there. The one good thing that came of her being off of work was that she was able to volunteer at the food bank a lot more. They were appreciative of the help.

Before it was time to go, Kali carefully got dressed in the outfit she'd picked out for the day. Ashley said it was important to look competent, but not like she was trying too hard – she reasoned that wearing a suit or something would send the message that she was guilty.

Once she unburied her car from the snow, she drove to the hospital and found her way to the room where the hearing would be. It seemed that she wasn't the only person in trouble. She stood outside of the door with a man and another woman – they made pleasant conversation, though none of them mentioned what they were in for.

Finally, six minutes past nine, they were invited into the room. They took their seats together and watched as other people milled about chatting, grabbing coffee or snacking on the hospital provided baked goods. It all seemed too laid back to Kali. The most important thing in her life was on the line, and they not only started late, but did so to chit chat and eat stale breakfast pastries.

The head of the committee, a hospital administrator named Bruce Carmen, called the meeting to order at 9:09. Not quite ten minutes late, Kali observed, but may as well have been. He briefly read over the minutes of the last meeting, adding a joke that only he laughed at. He then went through and introduced the three defendants (he called them "guests") that were there that morning.

The man was up first. He slowly rose from his chair and took the hot seat in front of the panel. Kali listened anxiously, trying to work out the personalities of those sitting on the committee. She ignored the smug glances from Betsy, who also came to the hearing. Kali realized that it was probably to testify against her or to request that she get the death penalty.

They went over the man's case, asking him to explain what he'd done wrong. He admitted to falsifying the medical record – well, sort of. He explained that to save time, he documented and scanned all of his medications as "given" at once, instead of scanning them one by one as they were passed.

The committee did not take kindly to this. They told him that what he was doing, bypassing the safety measures of scanning the medications, put everyone at risk. They sentenced him (or instructed him, really, it wasn't a court of law) that he'd need to go through some re-education and have supervision for a month afterwards.

Kali tried to keep her jaw from dropping. She knew *tons* of nurses who did that when they were in a hurry. And nurses were often in a hurry. Why was this guy getting the book thrown at him?

Next, the other woman was called up. Her offense? Bad mouthing a coworker in a rant on Facebook. One of the committee members read her Facebook post, flat voiced, and then stared at her blankly. She started to cry, saying it was done in a moment of anger. She apologized and said it would never happen again.

The committee deliberated and decided that she would also need to go through re-education, and she was encouraged to delete her Facebook account entirely. She said that she would.

Kali gritted her teeth. If they overreacted to an online rant (that didn't even mention the coworker by name or anything!) they were *not* going to like what she had to say.

The woman left the room, clearly holding back more tears, and Kali took the hot seat, facing a long table of ten people. She sat up straight, shoulders back. She told herself that she would not let them make her cry. She reminded herself that what she did wasn't wrong – and even if she developed a crazy infatuation with Craig, that was not the reason she took him in to begin with.

"This one's a doozy," Bruce said. Everyone laughed.

Kali pinched her lips. Couldn't he try to be a bit more professional?

"Alright, Kalista Mitchell. Why don't you tell us why you're here?"

She cleared her throat. "Hi everyone. My name is Kali..."

Dorky intro. When she practiced it at home, the guy wasn't supposed to say her name right before.

Pushing away her thoughts, she continued. "I'm here because I was accused of inappropriate conduct with a patient."

He lifted his paper. "You were seen out on the town with this patient. Is that correct?"

"Yes, but – "

"And this was someone you cared for during your time in the ICU?"

She fidgeted. "Yes."

"Furthermore," Bruce said, slipping his glasses back up his nose, "it was suspected that you had the patient at your place of residence early in the morning?"

She scanned the faces of the committee members. All frowns. "That's correct, but – "

He sighed. "Is it correct that it was suspected or correct that it happened?"

"Correct that it happened, sir." She clenched her hands in her lap. "He was staying in my rental."

An audible gasp from the crowd behind her. Who were these spectators? Did they come just for the show?

"I had to take him in," she said hurriedly. "I ran into him at the food bank and he said he had nowhere to stay, that the men's shelter was full. And it was below freezing that night."

"Miss Mitchell, you are aware that people can take shelter with the police if needed?"

"No," she said slowly, "I didn't know that."

He nodded and wrote something down. Some of the committee members leaned toward each other to whisper. Kali felt like she was in that scene in Harry Potter where Harry almost gets expelled from Hogwarts for using magic to save the life of his mean, fat cousin. Except Craig wasn't mean or fat. She tried to brush away the thought and focus.

A woman at the end of the table spoke up.

"What was the nature of your relationship with this patient?"

"I provided him with shelter and food. I helped him find a job."

The woman smiled and said thank you. Kali smiled back. At least she got to make her case a little.

A man at the other end piped in. "It was reported to us that this patient was young, fit, and attractive. Are you telling us that your 'kindness' had nothing to do with this fact?"

"No," Kali stuttered, "it did not."

"Really? Would you have done that for any patient?"

"I think so," she said quietly. Well, maybe not any. Some people were aggressive or mean. That wouldn't have worked, she was scared enough of Craig as it was, and he was totally harmless.

The man at the end scoffed. "And you want us to believe that you didn't see him in a romantic way? This patient who, apparently, and I quote, 'all of the nurses found very hot,' per this written report?"

A written report calling Craig hot? Wow, how he would've loved to hear that. Kali opened her mouth, struggling because it was suddenly so dry. This wasn't how she expected it to go in her head. "No," she finally said. "I mean yes – that's the truth."

He shook his head and wrote something down. Kali sat there, feeling cold, and small, and worthless. There was more murmuring from the committee. She stared at the ground. It was all over for her. She knew it. They'd probably recommend that she lose her nursing license.

Suddenly she caught a movement from the corner of her eye. The side door opened, banging loudly against the wall behind it, as though the person who opened it had hulk strength. Everyone turned to look at the intruder.

"Oh dear, my apologies! Did not realize that door was made of such flimsy metal."

She thought she was hallucinating. It was Craig, in the flesh. How did *Craig* manage to get here, of all people? Even her own family wasn't allowed, even Ashley couldn't come and she worked at the hospital.

Bruce turned away from him, rubbing his forehead. "It is rare that we hear such serious allegations, Miss Mitchell."

"Excuse me, sorry that I was late," rang out that plucky British voice. "But it seemed that I missed introductions. Have I missed the character witness part of the hearing?"

Bruce turned to Craig, annoyed. "There are no character witnesses. Sir, please have a seat."

"Ah, well then, let me introduce myself, since you seem to have forgotten your manners." He caught Kali's eye before walking toward the front table. "Some of you may remember me as the reportedly *hot* patient who all of the nurses were in love with."

Kali suppressed a smile. So he had heard, after all. How long had he been standing there?

"While that is all quite flattering, I can tell you that this nurse, Kalista Mitchell, decidedly did *not* feel that way about me."

Bruce's face twisted with anger. "Sir, this is the last time that I will ask you to – "

"My name," Craig said, speaking deliberately loud and slow to drown out Bruce, "is Craig Watson. You may know me as one of Britain's most eligible bachelors. Or you may know my family business in London. Or, perhaps, you may recognize me as the top donor to this hospital as of..." he looked at his watch. "About forty minutes ago."

There was a confused murmur in the room.

Craig continued. "I'm sure you got notice of it. I made sure that everyone received an email about the ten million dollar donation that I made, and a picture of my big, smiling face. Go on Bruce, have a look at your email and tell me."

Someone passed a cell phone hurriedly down the table. Bruce looked down at it and stood up quickly.

Bruce shot up from his chair. "We are *extremely* sorry, Mr. Watson, to have failed to introduce you."

"That's quite alright, I took care of it. Let me help you with the rest of your job."

Bruce sat down and Craig continued. "A few weeks ago, I was visiting Madison when I was knocked unconscious after slipping on ice. An ambulance brought me to this hospital, and I awoke under the care of nurse Kali. Does that match with the story you have so far in your report?"

"Yes sir, it does," Bruce blurted out, almost slurring his words.

"I was assessed by a physician who determined I was suffering from amnesia. I had no idea who I was. No identity, no money, no shoes in fact. And the next day, when nurse Kali found me wandering around a soup kitchen for my next meal, she took pity on me. Much as I do on anyone who has to work beneath you, Bruce. Do you follow?"

He nodded.

"Good. I did, in fact, tell Kali that the men's shelter was full – this was a lie, I am sad to admit, because I was afraid that she would offer to take me there. And I did not find it to my liking. For this, Kali, I do apologize."

Everyone looked at her expectantly. "That's alright," she said quickly. Kali was too enthralled by his performance to care. It's not like he knew she would offer him a place to stay. It was a very Craig type short sighted fib.

"Thank you, Kali." Craig smiled and turned back to the panel. "I did not expect this in any way, but Kali offered me her rental flat. She set the rules very clearly. She told me that if I so much as sneezed in a way that made her uncomfortable, I was out. She provided me with a safe place to stay, and food, and work. Just as she told you. Never once did her behavior even approach inappropriate. However, you certainly are on to something."

"I am?" Bruce said, face red as an apple.

"Indeed. A superior of Kali's, I believe her name was Betsy, took a picture of us when Kali graciously offered to buy me some clothing at the thrift store. She then used this photograph to blackmail Kali into picking up shifts and working extra for the next few weeks."

The committee murmured again.

"And I don't have the documentation in front of me, but I would bet *ten million dollars* that Betsy was the one who reported Kali to your ethics committee. And I'll tell you what Bruce, it both-ered me so much that the woman who saved my life was under fire from her extortioner that I had to fly over here and see for myself."

Bruce stared at him for a moment, almost as though he were afraid to speak out of turn. Finally, he spoke. "Mr. Watson, first, please let me say what an *honor* it is to have you here."

Craig nodded and walked over to Kali, stopping once he stood at her side. "Sure thing, Bruce. I believe you have enough evidence to speak to your committee, wouldn't you agree?"

"Yes, of course."

The members all stood and huddled around Bruce this time. The crowd behind them whispered excitedly. Kali couldn't believe what was going on. She half wondered if she'd fainted and was dreaming all of this.

"Are you doing alright?" Craig asked her quietly.

She nodded. "Yes. Somehow things started turning around for me when you came in."

"Funny how that happened," he said with a smile.

The committee returned to their seats and Bruce cleared his throat.

"Again, Mr. Watson, thank you for taking the time to visit our hospital. We are so pleased to hear that you received such great care here."

"Right," Craig responded, stare fixed on Bruce.

"We are happy to report that this misunderstanding with nurse Kalista Mitchell is completely cleared. The committee agrees that she acted honorably and went above and beyond to ensure your safe care."

Kali felt a weight lifted from her chest. She wanted to yell out but didn't want to push her luck.

"Terrific to hear," Craig said. "Thank you, committee, for your fair judgement. Oh – and don't forget to address Betsy at your next meeting."

The room erupted with excited voices. Kali looked back at Betsy to see her grabbing her things in a huff as she stormed out of the room. It was loud enough now that she felt she could talk to Craig without being overheard.

"I can't believe any of this," she said.

"Are you ready to go then? Perhaps we can swing by Mac-Donald's?" Craig asked her.

She grinned at him. "Sure. I'm buying."

# Chapter 24

They got to the door and Craig paused. He wasn't done with Bruce quite yet.

"You go ahead, I'll catch up."

Kali nodded. "I'm going to call my mom."

"Good idea."

He watched as one of the committee members pulled her aside; from her facial expression, she appeared to be praising Kali quite heavily. Craig smiled to himself – Kali deserved better than that hearing, but it was the best he could do on short notice. He was pleased, at least, with the outcome.

He found Bruce piling up some papers and chatting with the other members of the committee. As soon as he saw Craig, his face started turning red again. Craig reminded himself to keep the disdain out of his voice. It was hard to do that with a man like Bruce, a man who grovelled to those he perceived to be more powerful and spat on those he thought were powerless.

There was such joy in his round little face earlier in the hearing. At first, Craig hoped that he may not need to step in, that perhaps they'd reach the right conclusion on their own. As soon as the questioning started, however, it was clear that Bruce made his mind up long ago. Craig frantically tried to pull the door open, then realized it was a "push" and not a "pull." It made for a dramatic entrance, at least.

"Mr. Watson, thank you again for taking the time out of your busy schedule to visit our hospital."

"Unfortunately, Bruce, I'd have preferred to not have to make either of these visits. Though I suppose no one ever *wants* to go to hospital, do they?"

Bruce laughed heartily. "Absolutely, that is *so* insightful."

Craig couldn't help but frown. "Right, well Bruce, I trust that you will resolve the issue of Kali's recent suspension."

"Of course, sir, I will do everything in my power to – "

"I suspect that she was unpaid during this rather long wait for a hearing?"

"I'm not sure, sir," he stammered, "perhaps unpaid or utilizing her time off to – "

Craig had no patience for him. "Now that she's been found to be sort of a hero, I understand that all of her wages and time off will be repaid to her?"

"Absolutely sir, I will see to it myself."

"Excellent Bruce. I didn't catch your last name?"

"Carmen – I have a bit of English ancestry myself, in fact."

Craig was not interested in the man's history. He wanted Bruce to know that he knew how to play his little game, too, and would come looking for him if anything went amiss. "Bruce Carmen. A name I won't forget. Thanks Bruce, have a nice day."

Craig went into the hallway in search of Kali. She was just finishing up her phone call.

"Alright mom, I'll let him know. Yes...okay, sure. I will." She mouthed a sorry to him.

He shook his head and whispered, "No problem."

Craig was happy to have an excuse to stand close to her and take in the lovely scent of her perfume. She looked as radiant as ever, except maybe a bit more weary after the interrogation. She looked so small and defenseless in front of that panel. What a joke that was. He wanted to flip the table and throw Bruce out of the window. Luckily it didn't come to that. The headlines would've been confusing. "Bad Boy Billionaire Terrorizes American Hospital, Throws Administrator into Bushes."

Kali tucked her phone into her purse. "My mom says 'hi' and sends a thousand thank you's."

"It was the least I could do," he said. "I'm sorry I didn't come sooner. I didn't know about the hearing until – "

"I didn't want to bother you with it," she said.

He sighed. "I'm glad I could help. And I'm glad that Ashley told my mum about it."

They stood awkwardly for a moment. Craig was so focused on what to say during her hearing that he hadn't had time to think of what to say after. There were so many things that he wanted to tell her – he didn't know where to start.

"Did you want to get some breakfast?" she asked.

"That would be lovely."

They walked out to the parking lot and Kali asked him if he had a car there as well.

"No, actually, I took a cab straight from the airport. Do you mind giving me a ride?"

She laughed. "For old times sake, sure."

Old times – did she already think that the weeks they spent together were history? It did seem like it was quite a long time ago, but Craig remembered them so vividly. It was the beginning of his life, really, the first time that he saw her face.

He got into her old Civic and somehow it felt more like home to him than any of the cars he had in his garage in London. Though it was cramped and had fur floating around, it felt just right. His soul felt a little lighter being back there with her.

She carefully navigated out of the parking lot and asked him where he'd like to go.

"Do you really want McDonald's?"

He shrugged. "Sure. I'm open to any suggestions now that we don't have to hide."

"I really can't thank you enough for what you just did. You saved my life."

"No, you saved my life. Literally. I merely defended your reputation in front of a panel of jackals."

Kali smiled. "Same thing."

"Is it?" He turned to her but she kept her eyes on the road.

"There's a diner we all like to go to sometimes after we finish overnights. Would you want to go there? My treat."

He suppressed a smile. Of course, she insisted on paying. "Sounds perfect."

The diner was only a few minutes away and when they arrived, Kali was greeted warmly and seated in a cozy booth. It was so like her to have friends no matter where she went. Craig suddenly felt rather nervous about what he wanted to tell her. She'd never actually expressed any romantic interest in him. In fact, she'd shown him quite the opposite interest. It seemed a bit of a stretch that she would ever see him in that way – but he had to try.

They looked over the menu and Craig insisted that she order for him, since he was sure that she knew the best dishes. After some argument, she agreed. The waitress took their orders and their menus, leaving them with nothing to look at but each other.

"How're your parents?" Kali asked.

"Very well, thank you. And yours?"

"They're extremely happy that I wasn't fired. So, again, thank you."

He smiled, keeping his eyes on hers. "It was nothing. Really."

Kali carefully picked out a sugar packet to mix into her iced tea. "And how's Bunny? Still finishing up last minute wedding details?"

"I have no idea," Craig said, sitting back. "Haven't talked to her in days."

"Oh."

He watched her. She stirred the sugar in rather deliberately – was she trying to appear like she didn't care? Or did she truly not care about his romantic life?

"The thing is," he said, leaning in, "that she's a bit angry with me right now."

Kali set down her spoon. "Oh no, for coming here?"

"No, for calling off the wedding."

She stared at him, wide eyed. "You called off the wedding?"

This wasn't how he wanted to tell her how he felt about her. She deserved better than hearing that she was the most amazing woman he'd ever met over eggs and bad coffee.

"I did," he said. "I finally remembered what happened on the night that I had the accident. And let's just say – well, she left me there. She made up that tale that I told her 'don't wait up.' "

Kali had a hand over her mouth. "She didn't."

He nodded. "She did."

"How could she? Craig, you have to be mistaken."

He took a swig of his coffee. "I am not, unfortunately. I believe it's for the best that we go our separate ways."

They sat in silence for a moment and he felt pressured to speak again. "I don't know who the old Craig Watson was, but the new Craig Watson didn't seem to get on all that well with Bunny. She seemed...more interested in the wedding itself than she was in me."

Kali took a breath. "Lots of women get very into their weddings."

"That's true. Though lots of women don't leave their beloved to die on a dark sidewalk."

Kali flinched. "I just can't believe it, have you talked to her?"

Why was she trying so hard to convince him that it wasn't true? Did she want him to be back with Bunny, so she wouldn't have to fight off his unwelcome advances? He decided to cool it, just for now. He had no idea how she felt, and it terrified him to think that once he told her how he felt, she might send him away forever. He wanted to enjoy his last hour with her if that was the case.

# Chapter 25

"I did talk to her," he said, leaning in. "She asked me if I expected her to nurse me back to health, or something."

Kali was trying *really* hard to not look excited that Bunny proved to be the heartless, snooty woman that she expected her to be. Her guilt over the way she felt for Craig was much diminished when Bunny was a crummy person – if she were a lovely, kind girl, Kali wouldn't be able to live with herself. She knew it was wrong, but her heart soared.

"What's wrong with nursing someone back to health?" Kali said with a smile. Okay, just one little comment. It couldn't hurt. Clearly Craig wasn't going to go from dating Miss Perfect Hair Heiress to a frumpy nurse whose car was covered in cat hair. She would've vacuumed it if she realized she'd be driving a billionaire around – the shelter had her run a lot of pick ups for them that past week and her car never looked furrier.

"Absolutely nothing, in my book. So I chucked her."

"Are your parents upset?"

Craig scrubbed his chin. "My father called her a 'rabid rabbit,' so – no, I think they were quite relieved."

"Oh. So they didn't, like, arrange the marriage?"

Craig let out a laugh. "This isn't the 18th century, Kali!"

She felt her cheeks grow hot. Of course they didn't. "Sorry!"

He grabbed her hand. "No, sorry, didn't mean to make you feel bad. It's just that – no, I made that terrible match all on my own."

She had to remind herself to breathe. His hand felt so warm and comforting over hers. She could go months without being touched by another person in such a gentle way. What an odd way to live, she thought sadly.

"Ah, okay, good to know that you rich people are just as bad at making decisions as the rest of us."

He smiled. "If not worse."

"So...are you flying right back home today?"

He shrugged. "I gave the crew the night to recover. So I think I'll stick around until morning."

"Oh, okay." Kali's heart started to pound in her chest. It seemed to be screaming "Come up with something to do so he has to spend the rest of the day with us!"

Kali's brain told her heart to shut it.

"Perhaps I could stop by and see Chip? He's the real reason I flew back."

She crossed her arms over her chest. "I knew it. You've come to kidnap my cat."

He squinted. "Not kidnap. Visit. Give him the option of choosing which of us he loves more."

"That's easy, I'm the one who feeds him."

Craig frowned. "Do you mind if we stop on the way to pick up some more tuna?"

Kali laughed. "Sorry, no stops."

They asked for the check and Kali made sure that she paid for it. She wasn't going to let Craig think he ran the show just because he was a billionaire. Kali wasn't some pauper – she could afford to pay for breakfast. Staring at the pile of potatoes, Craig observed that he'd finally found a place that served a more ridiculous amount of food than Kali did when making a lunch.

Kali drove them back to her place and when she opened the door, she couldn't believe that Chip was sitting at the top of the stairs, seemingly waiting for them.

"There's my boy!" Craig said.

Chip sat and stared at them.

"That's alright, Chip, I know how you feel about me," Craig said with a laugh.

"You probably smell different," Kali said. "Or he's just letting you know that he loves me more."

"That really hurts, you know. I saved his life. I was his nurse, actually."

Kali took off her coat. "How could you lower yourself to such a profession?" Oops. She shouldn't have said that. It was not classy to rejoice in a broken off engagement. But oh-so-hard not to say anything.

"I don't know what I ever saw in her," Craig said, shaking his head. "Anyways, can we sit down in the kitchen maybe? I have two things to give you."

"Uh oh," Kali replied. "Is it two fleas? A mating pair of fleas?"

Craig grinned. "No, I left them in your car."

They made their way over to the kitchen and Kali put on some water for tea. "I'm afraid of what this is going to be."

Craig pulled an envelope from the inner pocket of his suit. He looked so striking all dressed up – he probably scared the pants off of Bruce. Good.

"First, I have the money I owe you for room, board, and cloth-ing. I believe we agreed on a 200% interest rate?"

"Oh please don't," Kali said, crossing her arms. "You don't have to repay me, it was nothing. And I'm still not renting out the basement, I've been too lazy to take pictures so it's not even like it was a real rental."

"I insist. I did the math here," he pulled out another sheet covered with calculations. "I believe you'll find them to your liking."

Kali rolled her eyes but accepted the sheet. He charged himself $150 a day for the room and $20 a day for food.

"You were not eating twenty dollars worth of eggs and turkey sandwiches a day," Kali said.

He shrugged. "I rounded up."

Her eyes skipped over the rest of the calculations. "What is this? A general nursing fee?"

"Yes, that was for your professional opinion about my medical condition."

She laughed. This was so ridiculous. Her eyes landed on the bottom total. "Twelve thousand dollars? Are you *insane?* I absolutely will not accept that!"

"That's too bad, because I have a cashier's check with your name on it." He slipped it across the table.

"Craig! This is ridiculous!" She picked up the check, shaking her head, then tore it to pieces. She slid the scraps back across the table. "I will take your calculations and frame them. That's enough of a payment to me."

He frowned. "I thought you might do that, so I have *another* cashier's check right here..."

She covered her face with her hands. "You're kidding!"

"I am," he said, breaking into laughter. "But I did bring a second thing, because I figured that you wouldn't accept the money."

She crossed her arms over her chest. "Okay."

He slipped another envelope across the table. This one had gold lettering on the front: Kalista Mitchell, RN.

She shot him a suspicious look before delicately tearing it open. It was so pretty that she didn't want to damage it.

The letter inside read, "This pass entitles Kalista Mitchell to one roundtrip private jet flight to Paris, France with the guests of her choice. The pass includes unlimited nights at any Watson Hotel (penthouse suite exclusively) with unlimited room service and a daily personal driver. A private tour of the Louvre is also included for these honorary guests of the Watson family."

Kali looked up at Craig, hand covering her mouth. She felt a lump in her throat. How could she say no to this?

Craig broke the silence. "I dearly hope that you don't rip that one up."

Kali bit her lip. "Craig, I don't know what to say, this is..."

He took a step closer. "So you like it?"

"I *love* it! It's a dream come true!"

He smiled. "Good! I knew I'd get something right if I kept trying."

She ran her eyes over the letter again – she just couldn't believe it.

"Do you know who you'd like to bring?" he asked.

She took a deep breath. "I don't know! Ashley would kill me if I don't take her. And my mom – she's never been outside of the tristate area. My sisters would *die* to go to Paris."

He laughed. "Sounds like a nice girl's trip is forming."

"I guess it is!"

He took a step closer to her. "You know, there's a train that runs from London to Paris. I could pop over and help you with your sightseeing."

She scoffed. "Another Craig Watson city tour?"

He nodded. "You should know that I don't just offer that to anybody."

She felt butterflies raging in her stomach. Her heart got her to speak before her brain could stop it. "I would love that."

He took a step closer to her. "You know – I've been meaning to talk to you about Chip."

She looked up at him, puzzled. "Why?"

"It just seems that – the way he greeted me today, it was like he was mad at us."

"Because we didn't get him tuna?"

He laughed. He seemed nervous. "No, not that. Because we're his – you know, we're his people. And we're not together anymore. I think he liked us better when we were together."

Suddenly she understood what he was saying. Except she didn't really understand, because it didn't make any sense. Not to her brain, at least. While it was whizzing away, trying to figure out what was going on, her heart jumped with joy. "Oh, really?"

He took another step towards her, so they were almost touching. "Really."

Her brain caught up. She took a step back. "I don't – I can't, Craig."

"Why not?" he said softly.

What kind of a question was that? How could he even ask that, there was no answer to a question like that! After a moment, she said, "Because – I'm still not over Luke. And I'll never be over Luke. I will always love him. And that's not fair to anyone else, there's not..." Her voice trailed off. What else was there to say?

His stare was unbroken. "I didn't ask you to stop loving him. Why would I ever want to limit that big heart of yours?"

Kali felt tears welling up in her eyes. "I don't know if..."

In one swift motion, Craig had both of her hands in his. "Hey, don't cry. Please don't cry. I didn't mean to upset you. I know you'll always love him. But Kali, I just couldn't go back without telling you the truth." He squeezed her hands. "You saved me not just from the cold, but from myself. If it weren't for you, I'd be marrying a monster next month, and I was rather a selfish monster myself. But you changed me. You changed everything. Everything is better with you. I'd rather live out the rest of my life in your basement if it meant I'd have the chance to hear your laugh."

A smile broke across her face. "It's not even that nice of a basement!"

His eyes searched hers for a moment. "And...I understand how you feel about Luke, maybe better than most, because I know that I will love you until the day I take my last breath."

She couldn't hold it back anymore. She threw her arms around his neck and buried her sniffling face in his chest. He wrapped an arm around her and softly stroked her hair. She closed her eyes, just for a moment, to imagine what it would be like if she were brave enough to tell him the truth about how she felt. She wanted this moment to last forever.

A tiny voice in her head whispered, *It can be yours forever.*

She pulled away from him and took a deep breath. "I love you too, Craig."

A grin spread across his face. "Why didn't you just say so?"

She laughed as he swooped down and kissed her. His kiss was gentle, yet still somehow wildly passionate. She never thought she'd be kissed like that again. Kali thought her heart would explode with happiness.

There was a meow behind them. It was Chip, sitting atop the kitchen table.

"Chip! You're not allowed up there!" Kali said, shooing him.

Craig laughed. "I told you he wanted us to be together."

She shook her head in disbelief. "I guess you were right."

He looked at his watch. "I'm going to document that you said those words and have them framed."

"That's fine," she said, pulling him in for another kiss.

# Epilogue

On Christmas Eve, Craig's surprise for her arrived with a ring of the doorbell. She rushed to open the door, secretly hoping it was Craig himself.

It was a stranger; she tried to hide her disappointment. "Hello, how can I help you?"

She should've known better than to hope that. Ever since Craig took an active role in his father's company, there were certain holidays or weekends that he simply had to work. Kali didn't mind – he was incredibly happy learning about the business, and he never made a fuss when she worked weekends or overnights at the hospital. He was the head of the new US branch of the Watson Estates company, and he was in charge of building ten new hotels that year. She told him she'd let his Christmas Eve absence slide for that reason, but he promised they'd be together on Christmas.

"Hello, Miss Mitchell?"

"That's me."

He pulled an envelope out of his pocket. "This is from Mr. Watson."

"Thank you, would you like to come in?" she said. Her parents' house was crowded for the holiday, but they could make room for one limo driver.

"No, thank you miss, I will be waiting in the limousine whenever you are ready."

She gave him a puzzled look. "Oh, alright."

He went back to the waiting limousine and Kali closed the door. What was this all about? She hurriedly ripped open the letter.

*"My dearest Kali,*

*I've good news and bad news. The good news is that we'll be spending Christmas together. The bad news is that my mum decided to surprise you with a trip. Luckily, I think you'll like this one.*

*Yours forever,*
*Craig"*

What in the world did that mean? She looked up from the letter to see her entire family dressed in coats and boots, bags slung over their shoulders.

"What is going on?" she asked, bewildered.

"Oh good," her dad said. "You finally got your invitation. We've been waiting all day for that to come!"

"For what to come!"

Her mom stepped forward and patted her on the shoulder. "Well sweetie, about a month ago, Mrs. Watson invited us all to their house for Christmas. She wanted it to be kept a surprise for you, though."

"I can't believe you guys agreed to go to *London*!"

Marcy chimed in. "Are you kidding? After Paris, mom was *dying* to get out again!"

Kali smiled. They had the most wonderful time in Paris, even though at first her mother refused to go. Her initial argument was that there was nothing for her to do in Paris and it was for young people. Marcy and Ella Googled "things for old people to do in Paris," and found quite a hilarious list of activities. Her next argument was that she didn't have anything to wear – which Kali offered to help with because she too needed a wardrobe update. And finally, she said that their father simply couldn't survive without her. He stepped in and quashed that one quite quickly. By the end of the trip, she didn't want to leave and made them promise that they would make it a tradition.

"Well then...I guess I better grab my bag."

They all cheered in response. She ran upstairs, hastily repacking her bag before coming back down to join them in the limousine. She was surprised to see that the two family dogs also piled in with them.

"Craig said to bring them," her mom said sheepishly.

Kali laughed. Craig had such a soft spot for all of the family pets. He arranged for all of them to get pet passports so they could travel freely. Kali had no idea that was a thing until he showed up with them one day.

They settled into their flight, everyone abuzz with excitement. The flight crew handed out blankets and pillows before putting on a movie of their choice – Ella insisted on watching *Elf*. When the movie was over, Kali looked around to see that everyone else was sound asleep. All the excitement must've tired them out. She settled into her own reclining seat and slipped into a deep sleep.

When they landed, Craig was standing on the runway with a Santa hat on top of his head.

"Happy Christmas!" he said, hugging each person as they stepped down.

Kali was last to get off of the plane. She wanted to jump into his arms and kiss him all over his face, but she thought it might make her family feel a bit awkward. She settled on kissing him on the cheek and whispering in his ear, "I don't know how you managed to get them all here."

He pulled back, "You're not upset, are you?"

"No! I'm impressed. And excited. This is really nice, Craig."

"Good," he said, beaming. "Well then, onwards with the festivities!"

They split up into three cars. Craig opening the door for Kali to sit with him in the Ferrari. She mentioned *once* that she saw one on TV and thought it looked pretty. That was enough for him to ensure that he always had "a pretty one" whenever they went out. It made Kali laugh – she was still driving her Honda Civic at home so it was quite a stark difference.

It was nice to have a few minutes alone with him on the way to his parents' house. She got her chance to kiss him when no one was looking. He smelled heavenly – he was wearing her favorite cologne.

The drive went by much too fast and they arrived to find his parents standing outside, waving excitedly. Craig groaned. "I told them to stop doing that, it makes them look like loons."

"I'm sure they just want to make a good first impression. I hope they all get along," Kali added nervously. Though their parents had talked over video calls occasionally when she was visiting, they'd never met in person.

"How much do you want to bet that your dad puts on those fake teeth again?"

"He won't be able to. I hid them from him. Mum said he was looking for them all morning."

Kali let out a hearty laugh and got out of the car. Craig introduced everyone and then rushed them inside. "We don't need to be standing out here in the cold when there's a perfectly good fire going inside!"

Kali was in awe of the house again. It was fully dressed for Christmas – garland, wreaths, lighting, and some serious looking fake icicles that adorned various corners. It looked absolutely magical.

As soon as they walked in, Craig's mom rushed everyone over to the fireplace to warm up. After handing out mugs of hot cocoa with marshmallows, she wheeled out several food carts. One was stacked with cookies, the others with tea sandwiches and savory snacks.

"A proper dinner will be served in an hour, but I didn't want you to go hungry!"

Immediately, Kali's mom asked about the recipes of the various dishes, which Craig's mom was extremely excited to share. Kali and her mom insisted on helping Maggie prepare dinner, so they spent the next hour chatting in the kitchen. Kali couldn't believe how well they were all getting along – it was like Craig bribed them or something. Even her sisters hadn't argued since they got there, and her brother was fully immersed in conversation with Phillip.

Dinner was delicious, and afterwards, they gathered around the fireplace to tell stories. Kali felt full, warm, and happy. At first she was just relieved that everyone was getting along so well, and after a while, she even started to relax. It was exactly like she'd pictured it for all those years – a trip with her family where everyone could just be together. Craig, except for his one bout of amnesia, seemed to forget nothing – he planned the perfect trip, just like she told him that she wanted all those months ago.

Midway through her dad's story about the paper mill burning down, Craig asked Kali if she'd like to get her present early.

"I don't think that's allowed," she whispered.

"But if we didn't tell anyone? I can't wait any longer."

Craig was terrible with waiting to give her presents. He never managed to wait until the actual occasion, be it her birthday or an anniversary. "Alright, I guess no one has to know."

They snuck out of the room and Craig led her up the stairs. He made her cover her eyes before he opened a door to one of the many guest rooms. She couldn't help but giggle as she stood there, hands covering her face.

"Okay, you can open your eyes," he said.

What she saw took her breath away. The room was decorated from top to bottom with fresh flowers. The smell was incredible. A fire burned merrily behind her, warming her back. There were rose petals scattered on the floor. And also on the floor was Craig, down on one knee.

"Kali – each day that I'm with you is the best day of my life, and somehow better than the last. Every day with you is summer. You are my absolute favorite person on this earth, and I can't imagine my life without you. Would you do me the honor of being my wife?"

For the first time, Kali looked away from his eyes to see the ring. It was a beautiful, but simple, design. A single stone, sparkling in the firelight.

"Oh Craig…it's beautiful!"

He took it out of the box and slipped it onto her finger. "Is that a yes?"

Kali laughed. "Of course it is! Yes, yes yes!"

A smile broke across his face and he leapt up, kissing her. After a second, they heard a sound at the doorway. Craig gave it a weary look before pulling it open.

Behind the door stood both of their families, hushing each other.

Kali burst into laughter. "Huh, what are you all doing up here?"

"We got lost," her dad replied. "Looking for the bathroom."

Her mom gasped. "Is that what I think it is?"

Kali grinned, outstretching her hand.

"Son!" Craig's mom yelled from the back, "You've surprised us all with this one! And we couldn't be happier."

"I learned from the best," he said with a wink.

"I couldn't be happier, either," Kali said, enjoying the full feeling in her heart. "Alright, shall we all go and find the bathroom together?"

Everyone laughed and they headed back downstairs, Kali and Craig hand in hand.

# Author's Note

Thanks for reading! I'd love to know what you thought, and reader reviews are one of the most influential factors in whether someone will give a book a chance. So, if you've enjoyed this book, would you please consider reviewing it?

## Would you like to read my free novella?

Sign up for my newsletter and get a copy of my free novella "Falling for my Brother's Billionaire Best Friend." You can sign up by visiting: http://bit.ly/LoveNovella

# Introduction to *Doctor's Date with a Billionaire*

## by Amelia Addler

They say no one dies in witness protection – as long as they stick to the guidelines. But what if you had to break the rules to save the one you love?

Jason spent his life running. Starting at a young age, his father's crimes haunted his every move. When he gets the chance to testify against his dad, he takes it, along with a new identity to protect him from retaliation.

The last thing Jason wants is for anyone else to get hurt because of his dad. Unfortunately, when Dr. Alexandra Small saves his dad's life, she becomes a target for some increasingly desperate goons. Jason refuses to testify unless Alex is protected, too, and she joins him in hiding.

After butting heads, Jason learns that Alex has a hard time laying low. When a tragedy forces her to leave witness protection, Jason must choose between his own safety and coming to her rescue. Will he give up the life he's always wanted to save the woman he loves?

**Excerpt follows:**

# Chapter 1

Jason looked at his watch and sighed. His dad was late, as usual. He tried to focus on the menu and decide on lunch, but he kept catching himself looking around the restaurant instead; he was worried he'd been followed.

Nobody looked suspicious, and truth be told, he didn't know what he would do if there *was* someone suspicious. It made him nervous nevertheless.

After what felt like an eternity, Marty "Make it Happen" Brash finally arrived.

"Sorry I'm late," his dad said in a low voice. "I have to be extra careful these days."

Marty was out on bail, and in a few short weeks he would stand trial to answer for decades of financial crimes and fraud.

"It's okay."

Jason wasn't sure how to feel. Part of him hoped that his dad wouldn't show up to lunch. Then the only time he'd have to face him would be at trial.

"What's new with you?" Marty asked, sitting back casually.

What an absurd question. They hadn't seen each other in three years, yet he acted like they were just catching up.

Jason decided that it was best not to drag it out. "There are some things I need to tell you."

Marty peered down at his menu. "How's work?"

"It's fine," Jason said, crossing him arms. "Nothing exciting." He couldn't stand faking pleasant conversation with his dad, pretending that everything was okay.

Marty continued. "What's good here? Do you think the turkey burgers are decent? I'm supposed to watch my cholesterol."

"I'm not really sure."

"What lonely soul even came up with turkey burgers?" his dad mused.

Now Jason knew that he was stalling on purpose. "There's something I think you deserve to know. You've hurt a lot of people. And I've agreed to testify against you at trial."

Marty didn't react right away. He kept looking at the choices in front of him, eyes scanning back and forth. After a moment, he set the menu down. "I know, son."

Jason sat back, surprised. He'd dreaded having to say that out loud for the past few weeks – no, actually it was a dread he'd had for years.


When he was younger, he didn't realize that his father was actually a conman. At first, Jason was even unwittingly part of his father's schemes.

It started when he was in high school when his dad needed help with the computer.

"There are always problems with these computers," he'd say. "How am I supposed to get anything done?"

Jason showed him how to use a word processor and spreadsheets to keep track of things, including expenses, payments, and business partners.

Jason had no idea what any of the numbers or names were linked to. At that age, he didn't quite understand what fraud was. He didn't know that his dad was the go-to guy for white collar crime. All he knew was that it took his dad forever to do anything on the computer, so he had to keep track of everything for him.

As he got older, Jason learned that none of his dad's businesses or banking deals were legitimate. He quickly removed himself from anything to do with the "family business." He was ashamed that he was ever involved. After dropping out of college, Jason got an apprenticeship as a carpenter. He never looked back.

It wasn't until FBI agents showed up at his door that he truly understood the stunning depths of his dad's crimes. Jason wasn't in any trouble, and while that was good news for him, it made the agents worry it was a long shot that he'd say anything against his father.

When they showed him how much money his father stole, and how much it hurt innocent people who were too trusting with their savings, Jason was disgusted. He agreed to cooperate and offer any information he had. He couldn't live with himself otherwise.

Yet he didn't expect his dad to be so calm about it.

Jason broke the silence. "You're not...angry?"

Marty sighed. "No. I'm not angry. Not with you."

Jason didn't know what to say. Did his dad understand the seriousness of the accusations against him? Did he understand that with the evidence the FBI had, he would probably be in jail for years?

Marty continued. "Things got out of control, you know, out of hand. When you were little, and you don't remember this, I was just like any other guy working at a bank. And when I saw that there were chances to make more money, I couldn't resist. I figured that we weren't hurting anybody – just a few suckers. I know it's hard to believe now, but everything I did, I did because I wanted a better life for you."

Jason gritted his teeth. Was his dad trying to guilt him now? That would be a nice touch on their already delicate father-son relationship.

Part of the reason that Jason offered to help his dad in the first place was because he wanted to spend more time with his dad. He was always working, and Jason wanted to learn from his father and follow in his footsteps. He wanted to make him proud.

Jason shook off the memories. He was an adult now, and he couldn't let his dad play mind games with him. "Is this some sort of a trick?"

"No, no," his father replied hurriedly. "Not this. This is real. I've had a lot of time to think about everything – how I ended up here. Why I ended up here. I lost sight of what's important. I have a lot to be ashamed of." He paused to rub his forehead. "Long story short, I'm not angry at you at all. I'm only angry at myself."

Jason took a deep breath and sat back. His dad could charm his way out of almost any situation, but it really didn't seem like he was spinning a tale this time. It seemed genuine.

Jason studied his face. For the first time in his life, his dad looked tired. He had bags under his eyes. His posture was slumped. He'd always been full of life, full of schemes. Today, he looked defeated.

How long had he been like this? For the past few years, Jason pulled away from anything that had to do with his dad, so he hadn't seen him at all. He spoke to him occasionally, for holidays and birthdays. After years of trying to convince him to stop with all the schemes, he finally gave up. Eventually, Jason knew that his only chance at a normal life was to leave it all behind, his dad included.

"Okay then," Jason finally replied. He had no choice but to believe him.

A waitress stopped at their table. Jason put in an order for coffee and his father ordered a soda. She asked if they were ready to order and they looked at each other, wide eyed, doing that universal shrug as if to say "I am if you are!"

The exchange seemed so normal, so casual, that Jason couldn't help but note the absurdity of it all. No one from the outside would be able to see the cracks in their relationship. They looked like two guys having a relaxing lunch, ordering a pair of bacon burgers.

"So much for your cholesterol," said Jason.

His dad shrugged. "I'll do better next time."

As they waited for their food to come out, Jason answered what felt like a barrage of questions about his work and his life. It was like his dad was trying to make up for the last few years when all he seemed to care about was making more money.

When he was twenty, he would have loved for his dad to be so interested in his life. But all of this interest was about thirteen years too late.

After twenty minutes, their burgers arrived, stacked high and crowded with french fries. Jason looked around the restaurant – it didn't seem like anyone was watching them. The FBI agents warned him to be careful, but perhaps he'd taken the paranoia a bit too far.

"Now Jason," Marty said, squirting some ketchup onto his plate. "I know that I'll probably be going away for a bit. Could be the rest of my life, who knows how many years I have left."

Jason cringed. It was one thing to think about his dad living out the rest of his years in prison, but it was an entirely different thing to hear it said out loud.

He cleared his throat. "Yeah. That's what I heard."

Marty dipped a french fry in ketchup. "And I know that you don't agree with how I did it, but like I said, everything I did was for you. I don't want you to have to wait until I croak to get the money I've saved."

Jason set his coffee cup down. "Dad – "

"Hear me out," he said, cutting him off. "There's nothing shady about this. I talked to my lawyer and I can leave you *everything*. You won't have to work as a carpenter anymore."

"I love being a carpenter," Jason replied. "And I don't need the money."

Marty shoved a clump of fries into his mouth, chewing as he spoke. "Jason, I don't think you realize how much money I'm talking." He dropped his voice. "Two *billion* dollars."

Jason crossed his arms. It was more than he expected, but it didn't sway him. The higher the number, the more people his dad scammed. "I won't accept any of it."

His dad gasped.

Jason shook his head. "I just can't, Dad."

Marty shook his head frantically, pointing to his throat.

"Are you choking?" Jason asked, hearing the panic in his own voice.

Marty's face turned red.

Jason didn't know what to do. He stood up, darting to his dad's side, trying to remember what the procedure was in a situation like this. His mind was totally blank. He stood there, mouth open, gaping at his father with no idea how to help him.

Out of nowhere, a cascade of long hair crossed in front of Jason's sight. The next thing he saw was a pair of arms wrapped around his father's chest, the hands folded into a fist that thrusted under his sternum.

"Alright big guy," the woman called out. She continued speaking between thrusts. "We are not – going to let – you choke!"

A soggy clump of french fries flew from Marty's mouth onto the floor. He gasped for air and the woman patted him on the back.

"See?" she said with a smile. "I told you I wouldn't let you choke."

Jason stood there, his mouth still hanging open. His mind was too slow to catch up with what happened. He still felt panicked, even though he could see that his dad was breathing – no, laughing.

"Dad, are you okay?"

"Yeah, yeah, I'm fine." He dabbed at his forehead with his napkin. "Just tried to shove too many fries in at once, I guess."

He laughed and the woman laughed with him. She even let out a little snort.

"I'm glad you're okay," she said. "Does anything hurt?"

"Not at all," Marty replied, patting his belly. "I've been saved by an angel."

"Oh yeah right," she said with a giggle.

"You know," Marty said without missing a beat, "I always hoped my son would find a *strong* woman!"

Jason stared at him, horrified. How was it that his dad maintained the ability to completely embarrass him after all of these years? Was it like riding a bicycle, a skill he'd never lose?

She handled the awkward comment with grace. "That was my workout for the day, so thank you."

She smiled and turned to leave.

Jason wanted to say something, but still couldn't think straight. He was stunned with what happened.

She really *was* strong. And he was surprised that she was able to get her arms around his dad's big belly. She was tall, maybe even as tall as his dad. For some reason, that was all that his brain could focus on.

He continued gaping as she disappeared through the front door. The moment to thank her passed. Jason sat down at the table and focused his eyes back on his dad.

"One fry at a time, okay?"

"Forget the fries," his dad said, mouth full. "This burger is delicious!"

# Chapter 2

Alex rushed to her car. She was already running late before stopping into the diner to grab lunch, and then she saw that guy choking! She couldn't just leave him there. Luckily, it was an easy rescue. It only took a few Heimlich thrusts and the man was back to his burger. Alex stuffed the rest of her donut into her mouth as she started her car.

She got to clinic with just enough time to say hello to the front end staff, wash her hands, and check her schedule for the day. She was excited to see that her first patient was one of her favorites.

"Mrs. Higgins! It's so lovely to see you," Alex said as she walked into the room.

Mrs. Higgins flashed a little smile. "And it's always nice to see you Dr. Small."

"What brings you in today? Nothing wrong I hope?"

"Oh no, you know me. Tough as a bag of nails. A 90 year old bag of nails."

Alex laughed. "Yes, of course. But you know that you can always tell me if you're having any trouble."

Mrs. Higgins smiled. "I know, kiddo. That's why I keep coming to see you."

Alex completed a physical exam and reviewed all of Mrs. Higgins' most recent blood work. It was all wonderfully normal. Mrs. Higgins had nothing new to report, except for some pictures of her great-grandchildren.

Alex loved baby pictures. She oohed and gushed over their chubby cheeks.

Mrs. Higgins tucked the pictures back into her purse. "Dr. Small, you know that I worry about you."

"Me? Why?" she replied, though she knew what was coming.

"You can't be a day over 26, but you won't be young forever. Don't forget to find a nice man to start a family with."

Alex almost corrected her to say that she was 31, not 26, but she stopped herself when she realized that it would only make her situation seem worse.

"I'm working on it," she said with a wink.

Mrs. Higgins stood up and fetched a plastic container from her purse. "I made these this morning, just for you and the girls."

Chocolate chip cookies. Alex loved Mrs. Higgins' cookies, but it made her feel guilty that this sweet 90 year old woman was getting up early to bake for them.

"You're too good to us. You know that we all love your baking, but I don't want you to feel like you have to trouble yourself like that just to come in and see us."

Mrs. Higgins pulled her in for a hug. "Oh hush, an old lady likes to feel useful once in a while."

Alex escorted her to the front lobby, carrying the container with her. The rest of the staff spotted the cookies at once and demanded that she open them immediately. Alex obliged; she was happy that Mrs. Higgins could see how much her efforts were appreciated.

The rest of Alex's day flew by; she always liked coming up to this clinic. She was part of a group of doctors who traveled between a handful of the rural clinics in the area, and her schedule at this spot in particular was always packed.

After she finished medical school, she wanted to move back home to be close to her parents. She interviewed at several primary care offices in her hometown of Albany, New York, but none of them felt quite right.

The offices were fine, of course; the other doctors seemed nice and the staff was hardworking. Yet none of them had a mission that inspired her as much as the rural health clinic group – the doctors there traveled around to ensure that the people of upstate New York got the care they deserved.

It was a shame that there was such a shortage of doctors in the area. Her interview there felt like a dream come true and she accepted the job offer immediately. Alex was happy to contribute, even in her small way.

Since most of the clinics were north of Albany, she had to live a bit further from her parents, but she didn't mind. The scenery more than made up for it – it was an absolutely breathtaking part of the country.

She didn't have a chance to take a break that day until 5 PM when her last patient of the day was a no show. She was surprised; Mr. Willow had never missed an appointment before.

"Do you want me to give him a call?" asked Jean, one of Alex's favorite nurses.

"I would really appreciate it if you could," Alex said. "Tell him that if he's not feeling well, I can stop by on my way home and check on him."

"Okay, I'll let him know."

Alex wandered into the break room in search of something to eat. All she had eaten that day was half a bagel for breakfast and that donut for lunch. Her morning clinic in the next town over ran late, which led to a domino effect of lateness.

It was all for a good reason, though. Her last patient of the morning came in crying, devastated by the loss of her husband the previous month. Alex sat with her, holding her hand and listening to her. She tried to offer as much comfort as she could. Though she wished she could do more, the *least* she could do was share her time. Falling a bit behind schedule was a small price to pay.

The break room fridge had nothing but week-old pizza; Alex gave it a sniff and recoiled. As hungry as she was, it wasn't worth getting food poisoning.

She settled on pouring herself a mug of coffee. It was unfortunate that all of Mrs. Higgins' cookies were gone, because they would've been great with coffee. She wished she'd stashed one for herself earlier.

Oh well! There would always be next time. Mrs. Higgins insisted on bringing something every time she came.

Maybe by the next time they saw each other, Alex would be able to tell Mrs. Higgins that she was actually seeing someone. What would she say if she knew her real age? Or that she hadn't been on a date in years?

Alex knew that things wouldn't change on their own – she'd have to make an effort if she wanted a relationship. Or, for that matter, if she ever wanted to have the family she'd always imagined. There were a lot of excuses she'd made over the years as to why it wasn't the right time.

The biggest was that her job took up a lot of time. But she loved her job. It was always her dream to be a doctor, and it seemed like she worked her entire life to get to this point.

She had a boyfriend once – Brian. They met in college and dated for two years. He was a wonderful guy, and she thought for sure that someday they would get married and start a family.

But life doesn't always turn out the way that you expect. When Alex got into her dream medical school in North Carolina, she didn't hesitate to accept.

Alex didn't like to overthink things that felt right, and this definitely felt right. Brian gave her his full support, too, even though he had a job back in Syracuse that meant they'd have a nine hour drive between them.

She believed that she and Brian would be able to work it out. Their love was strong enough to survive the distance.

And maybe it was strong enough to survive the distance. But it wasn't strong enough to survive Brian's stressful job, Alex's constant studying, and Brian's mom being diagnosed with cancer.

After the first year, he told her that he just couldn't do it anymore.

She could have dropped out of medical school then and there, moved back up North, and married him. She knew, though, that if she did that, it was unlikely she would ever go back to school to finish her training.

It was one of the hardest decisions she ever had to make. She loved Brian with all of her heart. She wanted to be there for him. But when she thought about giving up her seat at school, she just couldn't do it. She couldn't abandon that chance to make her dream come true.

It broke her heart to say goodbye to him, but in the back of her mind, she always hoped that one day they would end up together again.

That didn't work out, of course. Alex pulled out her phone and navigated to Brian's Facebook page. She clicked on his profile picture – it was him, his wife, and their two beautiful children.

She stared at it for a moment, studying their smiles. She didn't feel bitter or angry. It's not like she didn't *want* Brian to be happy. He was a wonderful guy – he deserved to be happy.

In a selfish way, she felt sad for herself. It was sad that life made her choose between a great person, whom she loved with all of her heart, and her lifelong dream of being a doctor.

Mrs. Higgins was right, though. What was Alex waiting for? If 26 was pushing it for starting a family, 31 was practically ancient. If she wanted to have a husband and have little rugrats of her own, she needed to do something about it.

Alex stuck her phone back in her pocket. That was that. It was time to revive her love life. She wasn't sure exactly how she'd do it, but surely the first step was committing to change, right?

"Alex?" Jean popped her head into the break room.

"Hey Jean, what's up?"

"I called Mr. Willow. First he apologized for not calling us, said he overslept with a nap."

Alex smiled. "Oh, okay, I'm glad he's not sick."

Jean frowned. "He said he's been sleeping a lot lately, and that he's getting so tired because he can't catch his breath."

"Oh dear," Alex said with a sigh. "I wonder if his heart failure is flaring up. He might be carrying extra fluid that's making it harder to breath."

Jean shrugged. "Could be."

"Or maybe pneumonia again...he had it last year. He's still smoking so he's definitely at risk..."

"I tried to offer him some of the free nicotine patches," Jean replied. "He said he wasn't ready to quit yet."

Alex stood up. "Yeah, I remember. I appreciate that you're trying. One day he might be ready. Anyways – if you guys don't need anything from me, I think I'll stop over to his place and see what's going on."

"Sounds good, we're all set here."

"Alright Jean, thanks for all of your help today! See you guys next week!"

"Take care!"

Alex stopped by a computer to write down Mr. Willow's address before saying goodbye and getting into her car. Finding a husband would have to wait, at least for tonight. She told herself that maybe over the weekend she could join a dating website or something.

For now she was going to check on one of her notoriously stubborn patients and drive him to the emergency room, if need be.

***Doctor's Date with a Billionaire*** – **available on Amazon now.**

# About the Author

Amelia Addler writes always clean, always swoon-worthy romance stories and believes that everyone deserves their own happily ever after.

Her soulmate is a man who once spent five weeks driving her to work at 4AM after her car broke down (and he didn't complain, not even once). She is lucky enough to be married to that man and they live in Pittsburgh with their little yellow mutt. Visit her website at AmeliaAddler.com or drop her an email at AmeliaAddler@gmail.com.

# Also by Amelia...

## The Westcott Bay Series

*Saltwater Cove*

*Saltwater Studios*

*Saltwater Secrets*

*Saltwater Crossing*

*Saltwater Falls*

*Christmas at Saltwater Cove*

## The Billionaire Date Book Series

*Nurse's Date with a Billionaire*

*Doctor's Date with a Billionaire*

*Veterinarian's Date with a Billionaire*

Printed in Great Britain
by Amazon